ONE DAY
IT HAPPENS

ONE DAY
IT HAPPENS

stories by Mary Lou Dickinson

INANNA POETRY & FICTION SERIES

INANNA Publications and Education Inc.
Toronto, Canada

Some of this work was previously published, as follows: "Hello, Angel" in *The University of
Windsor Review* (1985); "A Country Weekend" in *The University of Windsor Review* (1977)
and broadcast on CBC Radio (1979); and "First She Killed Him" in *Writ* (1976).

Canada Council   **Conseil des Arts**
for the Arts   **du Canada**

The publisher gratefully acknowledges the support of the Canada Council for the Arts
for its publishing program.

Library and Archives Canada Cataloguing in Publication

Dickinson, Mary Lou, 1937-
  One day it happens : stories / by Mary Lou Dickinson

(Inanna poetry and fiction series)
ISBN 978-0-9782233-2-8

I. Title. II. Series.

PS8607.I346O53 2007   C813'.6   C2007-901946-3

Cover design by Valerie Fullard
Interior design by Luciana Ricciutelli
Printed and bound in Canada

Inanna Publications and Education Inc.
210 Founders College, York University
4700 Keele Street
Toronto, Ontario, Canada M3J 1P3
Telephone: (416) 736-5356 Fax (416) 736-5765
Email: inanna@yorku.ca Website: www.yorku.ca/inanna

In memory of my friends and mentors,
Adele Wiseman and William Kilbourn

Adele and Bill both paved the way for me with
their ongoing friendship and support.
They believed in me even when I did not believe in myself.

I regret that Adele and Bill,
to whom I am forever indebted, will not see this book.

Contents

Slides of Exotic Places

THE TELEPHONE RINGS, the first call of her shift.

"Distress Centre," she says. "Jan speaking."

Her watch reads ten after seven and she writes the time on a sheet of paper. Followed by the date – November 14, 1985 – and her name. At this time of year she often curls up with a book in the evenings, but she has chosen instead to offer some of her time to volunteer work. In her forties now and already a grandmother, her children are engrossed in their own lives, her job search for another position as a receptionist in a doctor's office is flagging, and there's been no man in her life for a while. Although she is still a fairly new volunteer, no matter how disheartened she feels or how lonely the callers are she seems to be able to make a connection with them. Often they thank her at the end of a call.

"You're going to be blown up," the voice on the other end whispers.

Her heart beats fast and her hands are clammy as she glances nervously over at her shift partner. Steve is cradling the receiver between his shoulder and the ear with the gold stud in it as he listens intently to someone. He nods at her as he fiddles with the twisted black cord, his hair falling over his forehead.

"I didn't hear you," Jan says into the mouthpiece. She figures she should be able to handle this unexpected threat.

"There's a bomb in your building," the voice repeats in the same whisper. "It will blow all of you up."

The voice is muffled and she can't tell if it's a man or a woman. In the brief instant she contemplates what it might be like to be at the centre of an explosion – limbs and clothing scattered and unrecognizable as she's seen at disaster or war zones on television – the caller hangs up.

1

Jan stares at the telephone, leaving the receiver off the hook. When the recording starts telling her to replace it, she shoves the phone in the drawer beside her. She believes it was a crank call, but she starts to shake anyway. Then she remembers the protocol for threats. Call the police and find the Director of the Centre pronto.

Steve stares out the window. Jan waves her arm, but he doesn't see her as he talks quietly into the receiver. It could be someone who is suicidal. It could be anyone. Her heart continues to pound as she dials 911. She reports the incident and is told the police will arrive soon. When Jan hangs up, Steve is still on the line. There is a poster on the bulletin board next to her desk announcing a gathering for this evening – *Slides of Exotic Places. Come one, come all! Staff, Volunteers. Tea, coffee provided. Bring your own sandwich.* She thinks the Director will probably be at the slide show.

Jan leaves Steve a note ... *A bomb threat. I've called the cops and I'm going to find Serge* ... and goes downstairs.

When she pushes the door open, she sees a bird with blue feet on the screen. The Galapagos Islands. Or somewhere in Central America. She wishes she could simply go in and watch. But right at this moment, she would rather be anywhere other than in this building. A bomb is unlikely, but not impossible.

Where is Serge? He must be here. The people in the room are shrouded in darkness, indistinguishable from each other. Except one man whose face is lit by the bulb in the projector. Jan is shocked to see that it's *him*. What is *he* doing here? Bob. She backs away, trying to hide from him. She dated Bob briefly a few years ago and when she refused to go out with him any more, he continued calling her to the point of being more than a nuisance, to being unnerving. Even after she asked him repeatedly not to.

There had been a dark leather couch with a red blanket on it in his living room. On their third date, before they had sex, he served her a meal of scallops and pasta and showed her the photographs of a trip he'd taken. And then, although she hadn't even decided whether to continue seeing him or not, he started to suggest reasons she shouldn't stay in touch with her friends. When she left, he said he'd call her the next day.

"Look, Bob, I don't think so," she told him. "I don't want you to call me again."

But he kept on calling her and coming around. And nothing she said seemed to deter him. Sometimes she would see his car parked just down the block from her apartment in a house near the Spadina subway station. She'd hurry to reach her lighted porch. Or there'd be a letter on the floor under the mail slot that didn't have a stamp on it and she knew he had been there, right on that same porch. When? She never saw him. Sometimes it would stop for months at a time and then it would start again. But it's been long enough that she'd thought, rather hopefully, she might be able finally to forget about him.

Now she has to enter this room and see if Serge is there and she's relieved when someone just inside the door asks if she wants something.

"Serge." Her eyes search the room for the Director. As she looks around, she sees an image of a nude woman on the screen and gasps as she recognizes herself. It's a photograph Bob took of her that last night in his apartment.

When someone turns on the light, the image on the screen disappears. Bob is leering at her and she tries to ignore how uncomfortable and creepy he makes her feel. She shivers and is relieved when Serge comes out into the passage with her.

"What is it, Jan?" Serge asks, closing the door behind him.

She wonders if he recognized her photograph on the screen. Breathing deeply, she looks down at the ground and notices that the laces in his jogging shoes don't match. Is he that absentminded? Or is he eccentric? Or maybe he just doesn't care about appearances.

"I had a threatening call," she says. "Someone said we'd be blown up." She tries to sound calm, but her voice is shaky.

"What did he say exactly?" Serge pushes his fingers through his hair as she repeats the words.

"He said there's a bomb."

"It's almost certainly a crank," he says. "Did you call the police?"

"Yes, I did. They're sending officers."

"Good work, Jan. Does Steve know?"

"I left a note for him. He's on a call."

There have been over a thousand volunteers at the centre in the years Serge has been there and he seems to know all of them. He can rattle off names and histories of both volunteers and callers, almost as if he carries around a "Who's Who" in his head.

Serge asks her to go from floor to floor and tell everyone. He says he'll inform the group watching the slides and wait for the police to arrive. In the basement there are three rooms that are used as offices, but they are all locked for the evening, he tells her.

Three people sitting cross-legged like eastern monks on a grey carpet on the top floor of the old building are the first Jan tells.

"Thanks," a woman says, her head shifting very slightly to look directly at Jan.

There's a blue candle on the floor at the centre of the room and a man in a sweater and jeans stares at the flame.

"Unless the police ask us to vacate the building, we'll continue with our meditation," a second woman tells Jan after a moment's quiet discussion among the three of them.

Back in the phone room, Steve is still talking on the distress line. He points to her note and signals that he will stay on the telephone. She finds Serge in his main floor office.

"I've talked to everyone," she says. "They all intend to stay. Which I assume is fine unless the police say otherwise."

There's a loud knock on the main door and two policemen enter. They ask questions and search each floor with Serge, like hunting dogs sniffing around and under each suspicious item. In the meeting room, everyone waits patiently with the lights on while one of the two policemen examines a knapsack on a chair and a plastic shopping bag.

"Who do these belong to?" he asks.

"They're mine," Serge says. He usually brings two large boxes of coconut and chocolate-covered donuts to gatherings.

"And that over there?" A large brown paper bag.

"Oh," Serge remembers. "The man showing slides brought it."

The officers check and find it empty. As soon as they turn to leave, the person nearest the door flicks the light switch and the people seated around the room go back to watching iguanas on the rocks of the Galapagos. It's as if no one even noticed the slide of her, Jan thinks hopefully.

"Why don't you insist that everyone leave the building?" she wonders aloud as they move out into the hall. "Isn't that what the police do?" She'd be very glad to see Bob leave, except she'd have to leave, too, and she might not be able to avoid him then.

"We have to investigate all threats," one of the officers says. "But we don't necessarily vacate premises. It depends." They don't say how often they are out on similar investigations, that the public would be more alarmed if they knew.

When Jan returns to the phone room, Steve has his feet on his desk.

"Yes," he says into his phone.

She feels vulnerable as she restores her receiver from the drawer to the cradle. The police have reassured her about the bomb threat; it's just another crank call to them. But now, she's more worried about Bob. She focuses her apprehension elsewhere when she picks up the telephone after two rings to a caller who says her husband has been arrested for cracking her ribs and the police have uncovered ninety-seven guns in the apartment.

"Where is he now?" Jan asks, her antennae rising. Could this scenario even be possible? But whenever she thinks about whether a call is authentic, she cautions herself. She knows how often she hears something startling only to realize how little she knows about the lives of most people.

"The police said they'd hold him at least until a bail hearing," the woman says. "When he's been released other times with conditions, he comes around anyway." A court order isn't enough to stop him.

Jan shivers as she looks up and sees Bob come into the phone room and put the projector under an empty desk. He smiles knowingly at her, then writes a note on a slip of paper and places it in front of her.

So you're a volunteer here, too! What a coincidence. I'll wait outside if it isn't a long call. So we can chat.

No, don't, she shakes her head. But she can see that he's waiting in the corridor near the stairs, his eyes eerily fixed on her. He must have known she would be here tonight. That photograph on the screen was deliberate. She feels far too visible and reaches to close the door so he can't see into the room, wishing she could disappear into the wallpaper. No one else she has dated ever questioned that something was over. Or tried to embarrass her. Other ex-boyfriends she runs into from time to time are often quite civil. With one she discusses the state of the economy, with another what new plays he has seen. There are men she doesn't acknowledge, like the lawyer from the early '70s who wore red jockey pants and walked into and out of her life on the first evening. She sometimes glimpses him on a downtown street in a tall fur hat, oblivious to her gaze. These are men, like Bob, who belong to another time in her life when she was able to live out the fantasies of a single woman, much easier before AIDS surfaced.

When she finishes with the call, she goes to the washroom. Startled to find Bob still standing against the wall at the top of the stairs, she retreats back into the phone room. He'd seemed an interesting enough man when they first met on the tennis court on a May afternoon long ago. He was looking for a doubles partner. A man with a slightly bizarre sense of humour, she'd thought, but she hadn't noticed anything that day that suggested danger.

"I'd like to talk to you," he says, his eyes looking her over suggestively.

"I have nothing to say," she says. What is more, she doesn't want anyone to see him talking to her. And especially not to hear him mention that photograph. Least of all Serge, a man who couples compassion with a relaxed demeanour and whom she wishes would notice that she's an interesting woman. Serge, she repeats his name to herself. There was a Serge in her high school class who became a doctor. She thinks his parents came from Russia.

"I was just about to ask if you wanted to join us for a beer in that pub up on Bloor Street," Bob says. "The one over near Brunswick."

"No, thanks," Jan says. He has to be kidding.

"C'mon," Bob says. "Give me a break. You never answered any of my notes or calls. How else was I ever going to find you?"

Jan looks at the craggy face of a fifty-year-old with a bald patch and a bulging stomach. "Is that why you're a volunteer here?" she asks. Could he have followed her here one day and decided to worm his way in as a volunteer? Or did he just happen to notice her name on the roster?

"So can I call you?" he asks.

"No."

There was a white rug on the floor in his apartment. A candle in the bathroom that he said he lit when he bathed alone late at night. She could imagine what he did then. Like the men who call and masturbate over the telephone. She hangs up as soon as she gets any inkling it's a sex call, but it's always disconcerting. Like the incredible array of garbage she carries from those years of dating one man after another, carving notches in an imaginary belt. She even picked up a man in front of the boats near the Empress Hotel in Victoria one spring. He asked if she were a tourist.

"Because of the camera," he said. "You can always tell."

It seems ludicrous now that she went with him so soon after the break-up of her marriage. He had a yacht in the harbour with a shag cover on the bed, which was where he took her after buying her apple cider in the house Emily Carr once lived in. She knew nothing significant about him. And yet he practically cried when she boarded the bus for Nanaimo en route back to Vancouver.

Then, as she stood on the steps of the bus nodding good-bye, he said, "I'm married. For the second time. And between us, we have five children. I made up the name I told you."

In some act of contrition perhaps, she doesn't know why, he sent her two bottles of apple cider on her birthday for years. She drank it, each time reminded of the yellow broom in flower on the rocks that spring in Victoria. And that she didn't even know his real name.

Serge comes up the stairs from his office. "Oh, Bob," Serge says. "You must meet Jan."

"We've met," Bob says.

Jan flushes and turns to go back into the phone room.

"Jan," Serge says. "Let Steve know the bomb threat was the work of a crank. The police will follow up on it, but tell him we have the all-clear now."

She slips away, hoping Bob will be gone by the time she leaves. As she finishes recording her calls and takes the loose-leaf to her shift partner, she can feel tightness moving up her neck and into her jaw. It feels as if her head will soon burst.

Steve puts on his coat and she follows him out into the hall where Serge and Bob are still talking.

"So," Serge says. "Are you two joining us for a beer?"

"I have a date," Steve says.

"Jan can't," Bob says.

"Well," Jan says. "Maybe I could." She feels suddenly brave; maybe she can go if Serge is there.

"The rain check is fine," Bob says. "I'll call you."

As best she can, Jan hides her dismay at the insidious way Bob has managed to create the impression they've agreed on something. She turns to take her umbrella from a hook while Bob goes down the stairs. Steve waves at her as he follows. Serge waits while the others disappear and nods at Jan's replacement as she enters the phone room. Jan glances at the roster tacked to the bulletin board by the door and notices that there are three Bobs. Bob 50, Bob 103, Bob 166.

The ache has spread to her eyes and the back of her head now, creeping toward her skull.

"Let me walk you to the subway, Jan," Serge says kindly. "You've had a rough night."

Jan doesn't ask why he didn't leave with the others. "I live within walking distance," she says.

"Well, let me walk part way with you," he says. "I'll forego the beer."

As they cross the square outside and the streetcar tracks on College Street, he takes her arm gently. "We need some extra help in the office," he says. "Are you interested?"

Jan can't think about anything except getting home and taking a bath and doing some exercises. Her head is throbbing.

"It's the roster," Serge says. "You get along well with people and you don't crack under pressure. The atmosphere is important for the volunteers."

"When do you need someone?" The thought of doing the overnights when someone cancels isn't something she relishes, although she's been looking for work for weeks now.

"Tomorrow."

"Tomorrow?" she says. "Tomorrow?"

"Well, I suppose we could wait until the next day."

"All right." She feels a twinge of excitement at the prospect of working again. Even though it isn't quite like any other job she's held in offices across the city.

"Great," he says.

It's only as Serge lopes off, moving nimbly through the people toward the subway, that Jan wonders what he'll say when he finds out the photograph Bob showed was of her taken in his apartment. She asked Bob to destroy them the last time she saw him and he gave her a handful of slides, watched through narrowed eyes as she held a match to them. But obviously he filed at least one away. Unpredictable, he keeps her unsettled. So, she's apprehensive when, two days later, she walks over to begin her new job.

A volunteer doing her first shift arrives breathlessly at Jan's desk moments after she sits down and asks her to pick up a call from the police station.

"Have there been any more threats?" the sergeant asks.

"I don't think so," Jan says.

She sees Serge's head as he comes up the stairs and she beckons to him. As soon as he takes the receiver, she gives the young volunteer a cup of coffee and an Oreo cookie. The woman has long, frizzy hair, tips bleached, green eyes wide and sparkling. When Serge hangs up, he exchanges a few words with the volunteer who smiles and heads upstairs to the phone room.

"Okay now?" Serge asks Jan, opening a drawer to show her a file that contains information for the roster.

"I think I know who made that threat," he says. "He could be charged. He will be if he does it again and I discover it's him."

"How would you know?" Jan asks.

"There are a couple of callers who are known to us. We've kept the information in case they cause problems. If it's who I think it is he'll likely call and start to brag about it before too long. This man has a history."

"What kind of creep would want to frighten people who are there to help him?" Jan says.

"Good question."

Jan studies the roster. Some names are marked "okay" and some aren't. She starts to call the unmarked ones to confirm shifts for the next week, managing to reach three answering machines, a woman with flu, and one busy signal. A juggling act. She is about to call a replacement for the sick woman when the phone rings.

"What are you doing there?" Bob asks.

"I work here," she said.

"I didn't know that." He asks for Serge.

"Before I get him, could you do a shift on Thursday?"

"Not this week," he says.

She turns to tell Serge the call is for him, "Bob 103," but he signals that he's on another line. Take a message, he mouths the words. Jan nods.

"I'll tell Serge you called," she says.

She ticks the "Please Call" box on a yellow slip. When Serge is off the telephone, he tells her a silly joke and then calls Bob. After that, he leaves to give a speech on suicide. The telephone rings again as he goes down the stairs, but by the time she races after him he's out on the street.

When Jan calls to check her home number for messages, the beep sounds right away so she knows there's at least one.

"Hi, Jan," a voice says and for an instant she thinks that it could be the same person who called the centre and made the threat. The same whisper. The same underlying menace. "It's Bob Watson." Did he make that call? Did he leave the slide show for a moment to call from a payphone? Why would he do it? It's ludicrous, she thinks, her imagination is working overtime. Will Serge think she's crazy if she tells him?

"I have your photograph right here," the voice whispers into her machine. "I'll put it on the bulletin board at the centre unless you call me."

How can she tell Serge about this? And whether she does or she doesn't, Bob is going to continue to make her life miserable. She recalls that he surprised her when he took the first photograph that evening and was unrepentant when she became angry and asked him to stop. He took a few more.

"You'll want them when you're old," he said. "You'll want to see that you weren't always lined and ugly."

So when Serge later asks if she'll come into his office and sit down, it doesn't surprise her. It's as if the script has been written and she is merely following instructions.

"Tell me, Jan," he says when she's settled in the chair he keeps for volunteers and visitors, "What do you know about Bob Watson?"

She blushes. She knows exactly what she's about to hear. "Those photos, he was supposed to tear them all up, but –" She has scarcely slept and all she can do is blurt out what's uppermost in her mind.

"What photos?" Serge asks. "I just wanted to tell you I could see you were uncomfortable around him the other evening."

"Did he show you the pictures?"

"No, he didn't show me anything."

"Well, he may. He took some compromising shots of me a number of years ago. He even projected one of them onto the screen the other night so that I saw it when I came to the door looking for you."

11

Serge shakes his head. "Don't worry about that," he says. "It's not an issue. Except that he had no right to do that. I also wanted to tell you that we've figured out that the threatening caller was one of the regulars. The police will follow up on that."

Jan feels relieved that that call is no longer connected to anything in particular. Until she begins to tell Serge that she's sure Bob is trying to intimidate her. She tells him about the message on her machine at home. "He said he'd post that picture of me on the bulletin board." Should she also say she thinks he's dangerous?

"I'm worried about him," she says. "It's been going on for a long time."

"It's going to be a tough one to prove," Serge says.

"So what do I do?" she asks. "Go into hiding?"

"Document," he says. "Document everything. It can be used to substantiate a charge against him eventually. It's difficult, but keeping a record will show a pattern. But the first step is to make sure he isn't doing shifts here any more. That's my bailiwick."

"How long will that take?"

"Not too long, but you can see that your paths don't cross by making sure you don't give him any shifts. You can say there aren't any at the moment. And don't worry about the photograph. I'll see to it nothing is posted on the bulletin boad."

Serge glances at an article on his desk and starts to flip through a stack of call sheets. What else can she say? She thinks back to one of the callers from the other day. She never saw anything as alarming as guns in Bob's apartment, but he hadn't needed them to create this growing sense of menace, had he? She will do what Serge suggested and document everything so she can go to the police. But she doesn't think she will ever feel safe again, at home, in the tub, in the shower, even with the doors locked. Every time her phone rings there, she will be hesitant to pick it up, afraid to hear Bob's sinister voice again. She will look over her shoulder when there are no other people on the street at dusk or early in the morning, afraid to find him hovering in the shadows. She doesn't understand why he's doing any of this. What she does know is that it won't end here.

"It's a tough one," Serge says, looking up at her from the clutter of his desk. "Keep me posted."

Jan nods and starts towards the outer office where her phone has begun to ring again. She reaches for the receiver.

One Day It Happens

As SHE PRESSES THE BELL, Libby notices a sign in the window of the Tremblays' house proclaiming support for the peace movement. It reminds her of the marches they've attended together at one time or another. Ever since they discovered that they lived on the same street and their children went to the same schools in downtown Toronto.

Through the tiny panes of glass, she sees a figure start to rise from the beige sofa as the chimes sound. It is Madeleine, Clare and Marcel Tremblay's daughter, who walks across the rug to the door and peers out before opening it.

"Well, what a delightful surprise," Libby says, the smile lines on her face taking over. "What are you doing here?" They are good friends by now, although Madeleine is young enough to be her daughter. Indeed, she is around the age of her own children.

"Between things," Madeleine says. She doesn't say anything about Marcel's heart attack a few weeks earlier, but it hangs there as part of the reason.

"Are you here for a while?"

"A couple of weeks. Maybe a little longer." Madeleine twists her dark hair through her fingers. "It's good to see you," she says. "Come in."

As Libby crosses the threshold, putting her sunglasses in her purse and unbuttoning her jacket, Madeline muses aloud about the time over ten years earlier when Libby visited the Tremblays in England, where they were living that year.

"Do you remember when we walked along the coast near Devon? Do you remember how we talked?"

It was Marcel's sabbatical year when Libby visited them. One day when the car was parked in Budleigh Salterton, they'd all had a picnic and she and Madeleine had walked together along a deserted beach that went for miles under the cliffs. They left Marcel lying on the beach, reading his book, wearing blue jeans with a large rip just below his derrière and socks with huge holes in them. Clare was sitting in a cranny in the cliffs, staring out over the water. It would be impossible to forget Madeleine's dark, quizzical eyes. Her dreams for her future. A diplomat in some African country? The ocean waves pounded against the red banks of the south shore as they walked. Madeleine was about twelve that year. She was forty.

"You were unlike any other visitor because you didn't just pass through," Madeleine says. "That year we spent in England, there was a constant stream of visitors. You were different. You came and stayed."

"I did, didn't I? I must have been enjoying myself." Clare made it so easy to be there and they went to so many interesting places, to Ottery St. Mary where Coleridge was born, Budleigh Salterton where Raleigh had lived. So although she awakened each day with the thought that this might be the time to leave, she never did. Never repacked her bag and headed out of the house with the thatched roof where she slept in the room their son, Jacques, had vacated for her, a room with heavy beams and a high white ceiling, a tiny window looking out over a field.

Clare appears from the shadows in the rear of the house. "How lovely to see you," she says, as if she's forgotten she suggested her friend drop by. "Would you like coffee? Or tea. Wine, maybe?"

"Thanks. Camomile or something like that."

"Will you take your jacket off and stay a while?"

"I can't stay long." She's on her way home from the theatre. It's always comfortable in their home, just as it was in England, but she has laundry to do. Dishes. A cat to feed. Phone calls to make. Bills to pay. But letting the inner cacophony recede, she takes off her jacket and Clare hangs it on a hook near the door.

On the day they walked near the cliffs, they drove back from the beach to their village through Woodbury hill castle, an iron age earth castle. Past a field where a bloody battle was fought between Protestants and Catholics. A countryside so peaceful, yet full of history extending back for centuries. In Budleigh Salterton, they saw a sign in a window that said, "No repairs to clocks over three hundred years old."

"I didn't really have any sense of who you were before that," Madeleine says. "I didn't pay much attention to any of the guests until you came. You even watched me and Jacques ride horseback. It must have been very boring for you."

"Boring? Never."

Libby remembers so clearly walking with Jacques through an orchard where she climbed a hill, walked through a field of pigs and climbed a barbed wire fence. When they arrived back at the house, Jacques said, "You passed the test."

"Thanks." Then, "And if I hadn't?"

"You'd have had to do it again."

She still marvels at the memory of Jacques's similarity to her own son, back in Toronto with his father. That trip was the first one abroad after the divorce. Time was hers in a new way. Periods when the children stayed with Barton and she went away. Somewhere different. That time to England where Clare had suggested a visit when she and Marcel were there. So, although until then they hadn't known each other well, she went. Every day when she came down to the kitchen, there was another picnic lunch and Clare suggesting yet another destination. Bath. Salisbury. Exeter. Southampton. And as the two women drove through the English countryside, they told each other stories and laughed a lot, before long feeling almost as close as sisters.

When Marcel wasn't teaching or writing, he and the children sometimes accompanied them. Then there was the day they walked on the moors and Marcel suddenly crashed down into a hidden ravine and hit his head.

"Marcel's fallen!" Clare exclaimed, dropping her bag and starting towards the gulch into which he'd disappeared. He could have been killed that day. But after he sat for a while huddled under the grey wool poncho Clare wrapped around him, he walked along almost as if nothing had happened. Perhaps a little more slowly, his face somewhat ashen. Clare insisted that he see a doctor the next day, but other than commenting on a sore leg and a few bruises, Marcel went on as usual.

"How was the play?" Clare asks, suddenly remembering with a wry smile. "Weren't you at the Tarragon?"

"I was. And the play was entertaining and witty and the acting convincing."

"Did you know that the brother of the actress who plays the lead role killed a woman?" Clare asks.

"Killed a woman?"

"Yes," Clare says. "That's all I know, but you wonder how she can live with knowing everyone who sees her name must think of that." In the ensuing silence – what is there to say after all? – Clare goes to the back of the house and Libby hears the clatter of dishes in the kitchen. The living room is quiet until Clare returns, carrying a plate of chocolate chip cookies.

"We saw plays in Devon, too," Madeleine says. "Do you remember when the villagers put on that evening's entertainment and the butcher played the lead role?"

"I remember."

Clare sits down in a chair and begins rocking, glancing upwards as footsteps descend. Madeleine does also. It's Marcel. He sprawls on the sofa with his reading glasses perched on the end of his nose, a newspaper spread out beside him. There are holes in the feet of both socks. Maybe he likes socks like that. Or else gets attached to them. More likely, he just doesn't notice.

Marcel looks around at all of them. "Do any of you know what the odds are of a woman being raped in the United States?" he asks.

Since they lived in England that year, Marcel's hair has receded and is almost white. Indeed many things have happened to all of them. All their children are on their own now or married and Clare and Marcel have their first grandchild. Yet although he's had the heart attack just a few weeks earlier, Marcel looks much the same.

"One in twenty thousand," Madeleine says.

"I have no idea," Libby says. "Lower than that I would imagine." What strikes her is that Marcel is reading the *New York Sunday Times* the way he read *The Economist* and the *Times Literary Supplement* in England. She has his last copy of the *Canadian Forum* so she knows he reads that also. She wonders what he'll read in France where he and Clare intend to spend his next sabbatical. She wonders if they'll make it to France.

"No," he says, his expression revealing that the actual statistic will astound them. His eyebrows are lifted and he peers around the room. "One in twelve," he says. "And for a black woman, one in eight."

They gasp.

"And the chances of being murdered in America are one in one hundred and thirty four."

"I don't know many people who are dead," Madeleine says. "I bet I could count them all on one hand." She proceeds to do so and gets up to six.

No one else counts.

"What astounds me is that I know four people who were murdered," Clare says. "And that's in Canada."

Marcel says he finds it more shocking to hear someone has committed suicide. "How many people do you know who have killed themselves?"

Clare knew two. They talk about them as if they are still alive. Libby remembers a friend who was found on a beach south of Vancouver almost twenty years earlier.

"I was devastated," she says. "She was a good friend even though she lived on the other side of the country then. She was missing for two weeks before they found her. We waited at Union Station that first weekend because Toronto seemed a likely place for her to come if she'd walked out on her family."

Some words from her friend's last letter remain embedded in her memory. *Deo volente, we will meet again soon.* It wasn't long after that letter that her friend overdosed on sleeping pills. She still wonders if she should have picked up somehow on that phrase. *Deo volente.*

And if she had, what she could have done, separated as she was by two thousand miles and the Rocky Mountains?

"This is turning into a morbid conversation," Clare says.

There's nervous laughter as they try to recall how it all started.

"It was Dad's statistics from the *Times*," Madeleine says.

"Yes," Marcel says.

But Libby ponders how often they do talk about death. As an abstract though. As if they are always preparing for the moment it will walk in and take one of them. And it has come close in the years they've known each other. Clare's surgery for a tumour which turned out to be contained, everyone distraught, Libby making soup in the Tremblays' kitchen to maintain some sense of normal as they all waited for the news from the hospital. Parents who have died already. Except Libby's mother, who often seems on the verge of it. The dreams she's had recently of planes that can't take off and are left stranded on remote runways.

"Why is the light on over the sofa?" Clare asks.

They all turn to look at the sunlight streaming in, lighting up the same spot the lamp does.

"I was reading," Madeleine says. "It was dark there until a little while ago."

"Did I tell you Jacques has found an apartment down in the Beaches?" Clare asks. "He's getting married."

"You know," Marcel says. "The only change I've noticed since the heart attack is that my extremities tingle more often."

"Which ones?" Madeleine asks.

"Oh, you know, fingers and toes. And you never really know if that's because of the drugs or if it's a symptom. I saw the doctor yesterday and I told him I sometimes feel light-headed when I get up suddenly. 'Oh, that's the drugs,' he said."

Libby finds herself watching Madeleine carefully. Madeleine is watching her father.

"He also told me it was too early to start jogging," Marcel says.

Madeleine doesn't take her eyes off him. When Marcel fell into the ravine on the moors, Libby had a sinking feeling as she helped Clare walk him to a sheltered spot. They could have seen him die that day. Since then, he has travelled to conferences in many places. Given speeches and seminars. Jogged four or five miles at least three times a week. When he collapsed at the door of the gym after a work out, they told him it was cardiac arrest. He doesn't remember any of it.

"It's as if it happened to someone else," Marcel says. They've all heard him say this often by now. "I'm planning to spend a week in Montreal," he adds. "I could be alone, but I'm going to stay with our daughter there. Otherwise, Clare and the rest of the family will worry. They're all worriers, you know."

"I don't want to know any more dead people," Madeleine mutters.

Clare starts to pick up glasses and cups from the coffee table and to straighten up some newspapers on the floor.

"I should be able to start jogging fairly soon, I think," Marcel says. "Except I do tire more quickly. The doctor wants me to do some stress tests."

"It didn't happen to someone else, Dad," Madeleine says.

Marcel just sits there and looks at Madeleine. He could say, "No, you're right, Mad, it happened to me," but he doesn't say anything at all. Libby wonders if he's ever read Clare's poem about death …

One day it happens and
the telephone rings. And what
do you say? What do you say?

Clare stands up, her face reddening, and takes the empty cups to the kitchen. Marcel goes to the bookshelf and comes back to the coffee table with a large map and some photographs. He hands the pictures to Libby, opens the map and spreads it out on the table.

"This is the house we're going to rent in Provence," he says. "See the clay tile roof."

While she looks at the photograph of a house with a cliff behind it and vines over the entrance, Marcel points out the location of the village on the map.

"You're going?"

"We're still planning to," Clare stands at the door now. "We'll see."

"We're booking passage on a freighter," Marcel says. "Madeleine says she'll do some courses somewhere in France so she can spend time with us. And all the other children want to visit. You'll come, too, won't you?"

"Of course she will," Clare says. "We'll take picnics to all sorts of places. Avignon and Aix and maybe even Le Camargue and Montpelier."

As Madeleine looks at the map from one angle, Libby goes over and kneels on the floor across from her. She looks at the topography of another country she has wanted to explore. Will they somehow meet in the little village in Provence, share picnics on country roads, explore hill towns, walk around the Roman ruins in some of the surrounding cities? Arles. Avignon. Will Marcel read *Le Monde*? And turn on the television to watch a play by Molière? Will he climb the nearby cliffs, urging them to follow?

Madeleine looks up and smiles hopefully. "Will you come?" she asks. "I'm thinking of studying in Toulouse. Would you like to walk with me in the Pyrenees?"

"Of course," Libby says.

Madeleine smiles as she curls up on the floor, those dark eyes piercing right into Libby's. For the moment, everything is all right. They will go to France. Libby will visit. She will stay for a while, not pass through in a few hours.

Madeleine begins to pore over the map. None of them knows then, nor can they, that within the next year Libby actually will visit Clare and Marcel in France. And she will walk with Madeleine in the Pyrenees. Indeed, although in the meantime her own life will take its own twists and turns, it won't be long until they are all there. Least of all do they know, nor would they have believed, that ten years later they will all, except Madeleine off in some country in Africa, be sitting in this same room. They will be sitting on the same sofa recovered with a striped heavy cotton fabric, bright new red and royal blue cushions propped up against the back. "Marcel and I are flying to Australia in the spring for two weeks," Clare will say. "Marcel will deliver a lecture in Sydney. I'm trying to line up some poetry readings."

Clare will have warned Libby when they planned to meet that she might have to cancel at the last minute because someone she knows is dying.

"You always know someone who's dying," Libby thinks. Or possibly even says. But won't add – "Or has been murdered."

Now, as she lies stretched out on the floor across from Madeleine, not knowing any of that, studying the map hopefully, what she thinks about are clocks in Budleigh Salterton that can only be repaired for three hundred years.

Hello, Angel

1.

PASSERS-BY ON THE STREET attracted his attention as Tom sat at his typewriter peering out the window. He could see a girl in a very short skirt with net stockings approaching the corner. At the same time as he hoped neither of his daughters (Alison was thirteen, Lynda seven) would ever dress to entice men so blatantly, he visualized the girl on an escalator in front of him. Would he be tempted to reach out and put his hand under her skirt? Probably. And as the girl walked away down the street and he watched her hips move in a gentle, undulating motion he felt his eyes cloud over. It had been so long since he'd slept with a woman (was it five months? six months? even seven?). Maybe he would go to a nearby bar later and bring someone home. He'd heard his tenant bring women in late at night. They stayed for an hour or so and then slipped out again. He could watch television and then go for a walk along the main street and watch the flow of people before he went to the bar. But the thought of going through with it left him empty. What kind of man was his tenant? It dawned on him that he rarely saw the man and knew even less about him. Even his daughters who were only with him on weekends seemed to know more than he did. He wondered if Marilyn would mind if he walked over to the house where she continued to live after the divorce, to see Alison and Lynda. Lynda went to school where a child had just recently been abducted from the playground. She had actually known her although they hadn't been in the same classroom. Now she had nightmares. He had been up with her on Saturday night when she slept over.

"It's all right, Angel. I'm here now," he had said softly, letting her head nestle against him.

During the week when his daughters were with Marilyn, Lynda wouldn't let her mother out of her sight. Apparently she followed her everywhere. Some days Tom thought it would be safer if they moved to the country. But was anywhere safe any more? He decided to call Marilyn to say that if she wanted to go out he would baby-sit. He would rather she didn't leave Alison, who was after all only thirteen, to do so.

"Anything might happen," he would say.

But he began instead to fidget with the paper on his desk and finally inserted a sheet in the typewriter.

2.

I heard noises through the wall that night, but I thought it was just another woman with him. I vomited in the bathroom right after the police told me they had found the body. He had raped her and strangled her and had put her body in a plastic bag and … Oh, no, it's too horrible. I can't stand it.

"Did you notice anything at all peculiar before the smell, Mr. N?" the tall cop asked me, peering into my room at the papers and books on my desk. At the newspapers overflowing from my bed onto the floor.

"I heard noises …" I began. "But it didn't dawn on me to call anyone until the smell started. When I began to hear about the child who had disappeared I remembered the commotion, but he had so many women in over the time he lived there."

"Yes, I'm a student," I told them as they poked around my room. I picked up the newspapers and piled them on the window ledge.

"Yes, I've been a student for a long time." They looked askance at my unshaven face and my blue jeans. Anyone over thirty shouldn't look like this, their eyes implied. I get that all the time. I'm used to it. I didn't bother to tell them about the prospecting job in northern Ontario or the time I spent doing research for the government. After a while, they left me to be sick at the vivid picture of the covered body being carried down the stairs.

Why did he do it? Did he watch her for a long time or did he just respond to a momentary whim that afternoon when he saw her playing in the schoolyard? I've watched children in that same schoolyard. I may even have seen her. She had long red hair tied back in a ponytail, or so the newspapers described her. If I had seen her, I think I would have remembered. Why was I watching the children? I was doing a survey for the Traffic Department at an intersection near the school. I had an official reason. I can't imagine that he had one. No, he did shift work in a factory, manufacturing something or other. Or was he a transient, lashing out in his frustration? Buried underneath layers of experience there must have been a reason. His parents beat him. He didn't have any parents and was shunted from one foster home to another. He hated women. He hated everyone. But is there any justification? Can there ever be? Did he understand there would not be when he stood and watched the sun pick up the copper lights in her hair? What made her stand out for him so that he picked her? Was it so arbitrary that it was merely because she was the last to leave that day?

3.

Tom looked at the pages in front of him, surprised at what he had written. He stood up and stared out at the street again, at a yellow Honda that was now parked at the curb. A small girl watched the driver get out of the car and Tom shivered with apprehension as he watched his tenant speak to her. A woman who appeared to be with the child moved out of the shadows. As she turned in a slow pirouette, the child smiled at the woman. Her face was framed by tawny hair and she wore a red plastic rain slicker just like his daughter's. Maybe the child who had been abducted had worn one. A thousand children must wear them.

As Tom turned around, he reached for the typewritten sheets and crumpled them into a ball. He would go jogging tonight, two miles at least. He didn't want this material which felt almost as if it had begun to emerge spontaneously from his typewriter, as if all he had to do was to feed paper into the machine. His foot throbbed as he moved across the room and he recalled that his doctor had told him to lay off the jogging. What else could he do? He hated swimming. He looked down at the paunch he was developing and sucked in his stomach. He would have to do something. He walked towards his desk like a sleepwalker and smoothed out the crumpled balls of paper. He didn't read them, but inserted another blank sheet into the typewriter. *Hello, Angel,* he typed in the middle. A title page. *Hello, Angel,* by … By whom? The story could invite murder of the "I" narrator. Some loony might try to kill him. But if he used a pseudonym, some innocent of that name might be killed.

4.

The description that was sent across the continent was of a man in his late thirties with brown hair, brown beard (has he shaved it?), rather stocky, around 5′ 11″. Apparently he had an alias while he worked at the factory and lived in the room beside me. I couldn't tell them much more about his appearance because I scarcely saw him and when I did, I didn't take notice. He was in the house for only a matter of two months or so and since he did shift work, he slept at odd hours. I saw him go up the stairs with women more than once, but he always shielded his face from me and, in any case, I would look hurriedly in the other direction.

Yes, this monster lived in the same house as I did. He ate and slept only a few feet from me, on the other side of a wall and a staircase. And in that room he murdered the child, without hesitation. Or did she frighten him? Maybe he didn't intend to hurt her. Maybe he only wanted some company for a while and became angry when she wanted to leave. How did he convince her to come to his room in the first place? In broad daylight would he have been able to force her?

5.

As he looked at the latest page sitting in the typewriter, Tom wondered if he would actually form it into a story. He wasn't interested in rape or murder and the thought that any man could molest a child sickened him. He swivelled around in his chair, searching for his briefcase. But he didn't want to think about the novel he had written. He had to make substantial revisions before his editor would publish it and he couldn't help but worry that he might not be able to do them, as he worried every time.

Above his desk, next to the window, books were piled haphazardly on top of each other on the shelves and as he reached for one, another fell into his hands. Kafka. *The Trial.* He hadn't read Kafka in years and he turned the pages idly and then moved around the room with a frown creasing his forehead. Finally he stretched out on a narrow couch pushed against the far wall where Alison slept on weekends. As he lay there he heard the front door open and listened to the tenant go up the stairs to his apartment. The man had lived in the house for about six months, but their paths didn't cross often. Sometimes he heard dishes clinking or a guitar playing, occasionally a radio. The man hadn't really said what he did when Tom had asked him. He speculated that if the tenant had been a criminal the horrible crime could even have taken place in this house when he was sleeping. He felt momentarily ill at the thought of the times he had left Alison and Lynda alone when sounds could be heard from above, thinking they were safer when someone else was there. Lynda wouldn't even have considered the man a stranger if he'd approached her, but could he have lured her into his room? What had made the child who was later found strangled leave the schoolyard? Why had she gone with the man? He walked toward his desk slowly.

6.

She's playing in the schoolyard, darting back and forth across the concrete. "Hey, I got you." "C'mon, you're It!" They laugh and play and run. They jump over cracks that will break backs. They skip rope. "Be home in an hour," her mother said. Their house is not far away and she can walk home alone. "Wait for me, Jen," she calls after a friend who runs off at the sound of a distant voice. "Jenny. Jenny." The friend disappears around the corner of the pale brick school. She turns to the others, but they have dashed in the other direction. She stoops to tie her shoelace and sees a man watching her when she stands up again. He peers through the link fence. If she runs to the gate maybe she can catch the other children.

"Hello, kid," he says.

She isn't supposed to talk to strangers. Her father has told her. Her mother has told her. The policeman who came to the school stood at the front of the gym and told everyone. Don't say Hello, Mister. Ever. But he's walking towards her. What will she do? She glances at him and he stops a few feet away from her.

"Sure is a nice day," he says. His smile is quick and friendly. "Catch," he says and throws a red ball with white stars on it in her direction. She's too startled to ignore it and reaches for it.

"Great catch," he says. "Here, throw it to me."

"Well," she says, then throws it and laughs aloud when he jumps for it. He pretends to throw it again, but she shakes her head.

"Ah well," he says. "Maybe you'd like some of these." He holds out a box of Smarties and moves a little closer. For each step forward she moves one back, but the length of his stride is longer. "It's okay," he says. "Here."

She puts out her palm and he pours the small candies into it. "What a princess," he says. "Where'd you get that pretty hair?"

She shakes it proudly and wrinkles her nose. "My Dad says it's because I'm an angel."

"Yes," he says. "An angel. Hello, Angel. How would you like to have some more Smarties? C'mon to the store down there." He points. It's on her way home and she knows the store. Why shouldn't she? Her father would like this man. She's startled when he pulls her up onto the porch of a house before they reach the corner, but when he says he wants to get his little girl and bring her, too, she thinks it must be all right.

"C'mon," he says from the hallway. "I have to wake her up. Come up and help me." He waits for her and pushes her gently up the stairs ahead of him. At the top, she's frightened.

"Where is she?" the child asks.

"Who?" His face is set now into cold lines that frighten her. She tries to squeeze by him to rush back down the stairs, but he grabs her and puts his hand over her mouth as he pushes open the door of his room. She kicks him and kicks him, but he is holding her so she can scarcely breathe.

7.

Tom sat back and gulped in a large breath of air. He could hear a typewriter in the empty silence, as if an invisible machine were continuing his story at a point where he could no longer bear to deal with it... *Hello, Angel* by Anonymous. He stood up and went to the kitchen and plugged in the kettle. He took out a filter and some Melita coffee and waited for the water to boil. The red numbers on his clock radio flashed. The power must have been off during a thunderstorm earlier in the day. There had been hailstones for a moment and then a heavy downpour. Or was that another storm earlier in the year? He pressed down the button that would stop the flicker and glanced at the pages of the newspaper he'd left spread out on the table. As he read his horoscope... *A phone call is lucky. Make plans to travel. You win a contest. Romance plays an important role in the decisions you make. A special invitation in the mail...* he heard the imaginary typewriter again and he listened to the even tempo of the keys striking the platen and the sound of the bell as the carriage reached the end of a line. After a while a chair scraped across the floor above and footsteps crossed the room.

The telephone began to ring and Tom pushed a pile of newspapers aside. The sound was louder, but he couldn't find the phone. He tossed books and papers until he found the receiver beside the couch, buried under another pile of paper.

"Hello," he said.

"Daddy?" his youngest daughter said.

"What is it, Angel?" he asked, a picture of her flooding over him. A smattering of freckles over her nose. A dimple. He missed his children desperately. Sometimes when he stood on the sidewalk and watched them walk back into their mother's house, he felt his eyes fill and tears slip down his cheeks.

"Mommy says can I stay with you this weekend when she goes away?"

He could imagine her face suddenly crease with a worried frown if he couldn't have her. He was glad he had nothing planned.

"Of course," he said, twisting the cord around his finger.

8.
In the picture pasted on poles all over the city, she had a happy face. A

smattering of freckles over her nose. A dimple. I would recognize that impish smile anywhere. How could anyone hurt someone who still had that ingenuous charm?

The schoolyard is just around the corner so I heard a lot about the case. Especially when the police trucks went by, blaring out her description, and the plain-clothes detective came to the door. If I had called them when I heard that scuffling noise and the incredible whimpering, would she be alive now? Would they have caught him? He was around for a few hours after that, but then no one saw him again during the days between the child's disappearance and the discovery of the body in the green garbage bag shoved to the back of his closet. The bag was on a shelf with boards up against it as if the closet were empty. In fact, until the smell started to permeate my room and a sickly prescience came over me, every time I saw the girl's photograph or heard her disappearance mentioned, I imagined she would appear somewhere and there would be a story about her running away from home in the newspapers the next day and the whole city would relax again. Yes, she would be alive and happy. I couldn't bear the prospect of her being any other way. The newspapers described the family, a decent, hard-working family with three other children. The parents couldn't sleep at night as they prayed for and worried about their youngest daughter. "I just hope they find her alive," her father said. There was no reason to suppose she had run away and he could only hope she wouldn't have gone anywhere with a stranger. "But she was seven," he said, his voice wavering. "Only seven." A friendly, curious child of seven. She might have stayed out longer than her friends because we told her to clean her room. Does he also feel responsible then for this monstrosity? Was there something he could have done to prevent it? How does one unsuspecting child become a victim? What sets that child apart? She was friendly. She was curious. She was seven. And a brute raped and murdered her.

9.

The next day when Tom went to the door to get his newspaper, the tenant was in the vestibule. The man pulled his collar up hurriedly and stepped out into a steady downpour. Over his shoulder he said,

"Lousy weather," his voice muffled.

Tom watched him rush toward the yellow Honda parked at the curb. Was there something sinister about him? A man with brown hair, brown beard, rather stocky. All morning an image of his tenant kept thrusting itself into his mind. At noon he went out for a walk and as he passed a store with a display of magazines in the window beside a delicatessen he frequented, he went inside. He noticed an issue of *Esquire* on a newsstand with an article about a killer in it. Although it repelled him, he knew he would have to buy it and read the article. He would have to read *Executioner's Song* some time also.

10.

At first it sounded as if he were scraping chairs across the room. Come on, man, I'm trying to sleep. Get on with it and get the broad out again. They didn't usually stay long and it could be quite noisy for a while. I used to imagine him in there with them, but I didn't think of them as women who might also have histories, only as food for his voracious appetite. But that he could harm a child, that he could take that helpless girl and force her to show him her body and then... No. No. He should be shut up in a cage with twenty locked doors between him and other people and ...

11.

Tom bought Lynda's favourite ice cream, mint chocolate, at the corner store before walking up the tree-lined street to meet her. He rang the doorbell and waited for the sound of her footsteps, but it was Marilyn who came to the door.

"She'll be down in a minute," his former wife said. "Come in and have a coffee?"

He stepped across the threshold of the house where he had lived for ten years and followed her down the tiled hallway to the kitchen. Alison had gone to a friend's house for the weekend, but Marilyn's suitcase was still in the hall. There was no sign of the boyfriend he had heard the girls mutter about, Clive something.

"I hate to leave her," Marilyn said. "She's still pretty upset. More than I think a child would be unless –" She stopped, her head turning suddenly towards the door. The sound of the toilet being flushed above reassured her. "Unless –"

"Unless?"

"What about the man who lives in your house, Tom?"

"What about him?" Tom said curtly.

"She seems frightened of him. Where does he come from? Who is he? What does he do?"

"I don't know," Tom said.

Marilyn frowned and turned to pour water from the kettle. "Find out, will you?"

"She seems frightened of almost any man now," Tom said. "Even Clive."

"Listen," Marilyn said. "As long as that maniac is on the loose –"

"All right," Tom said. "All right." A scene from the childhood of a future rapist flashed before him and he shuddered as he moved toward the door to see if Lynda was ready.

12.

The boy could hear the noises inside as he came up the street from school. He crouched down under the front window and listened. His sister was squealing and crying. "Don't do that, Poppa." He looked in the window and saw his father over her. "C'mon, you brat," he shouted, pulling her clothes off and forcing her down. The boy was afraid his father would see him and beat him again and crawled under the front porch until the man's grunting and the child's screaming stopped. What was his father doing to her? He felt sick and he didn't want to know. His mother did shift work and she was drunk when she didn't. When the boy was eleven, his father found his mother in bed with another man and tried to kill her. The man killed his father. The Children's Aid took the boy. He ran away from one foster home after another. He lived on the street. He scavenged. All of this happened before he was thirteen years old. By the time he was sixteen he had stolen a car, robbed a liquor store, and been part of a motorcyclists' gang rape. He wasn't caught again after the liquor store arrest because he was always on the move too quickly. He started to take new names …

13.

When they reached the house, his daughter grasped his hand. Her face clouded over.

"What's the matter, Angel?" Tom asked.

"Nothing," she said.

As they went into his apartment, she seemed nervous. "I don't like that man," she said.

"Which one?"

"The one upstairs."

"Why?"

"He has squinty eyes."

"Anything else?" Tom asked, his hands sweating. "Has he ever done anything to you, Angel?"

"Once he asked me to go into his place, but I didn't go."

14.

She didn't scream. There must have been a towel shoved in her mouth. If it had been his fist, she could have bitten him. He must have tied her hands and forced her onto the bed. She must have rolled and kicked so hard that it sounded as if he had been moving furniture. He hadn't intended to kill her, but had suddenly become frightened and taken a sheet and torn it into ragged strips and strangled her.

15.

Lynda sat at the kitchen table, her eyes following her father as he cleared plates streaked with spaghetti sauce from the table.

"Want some ice cream?" Tom asked.

"Yep."

"Too bad I don't have any," he said lightly.

"I saw it," she said, leaping up from her chair and pulling the carton from the freezer.

"Now that you're up, what about bowls and spoons, too?" Tom said.

As Lynda set the dishes out, the telephone rang and Tom listened to a friend say he couldn't come by that evening because his house had been ransacked earlier.

"You know that murder that happened near you?" the voice continued.

"Um."

"The cop who came to take the details on the robbery said the policeman who found the child's body has resigned from the force."

"Yeah," Tom said. "I don't blame him." He felt shivers spreading through his body and almost gagged on the ice cream as he sat down across from his daughter. He didn't want to think about the child or the murderer or the policeman. Why did everything remind him? But as Lynda wandered into the den to watch television, he wondered how to fit the policeman into his story.

16.

Insert in *Hello, Angel:*

He took away the board and found the garbage bag and peered into it. She was curled up inside it, absolutely still. Her red hair fell over the edge as he opened it. His voice rose in a silent scream. If he closes his eyes, he will see her. Whenever he closes his eyes, he sees her. Sometimes he is sick to his stomach. He has a constant headache. He awakens suddenly at night and breaks out in a sweat.

17.

Tom turned to watch the gentle rhythm of Lynda's breathing as she lay curled up, asleep, around a stuffed green elephant she'd had since she was a baby. He peered out again at the branches of a tree, at dark sky hung with stars, and listened to the rustle of wind through the leaves of autumn. The child wasn't the central character he was looking for. Nor was the policeman. He was drawn inexorably to the criminal...

18.

He knew he shouldn't stop when he saw the children playing because he had the dizzy feeling in his head again. It was the first time in a long time. He had hoped it was gone and would never come back again. When he had it, he didn't know what he might do. The last time, he followed a girl who got off a bus along a quiet street. He knocked her to the ground and raped her.

He had to hold his hand over her mouth and to push her head back to make her stop screaming. "Be quiet," he had begged as he found a rock with his other hand and started to hit her. He hadn't wanted to hurt her. If she hadn't screamed, he wouldn't have had to. He didn't have to hurt women who took money. They let him do it over and over until he didn't need to any more. That was all he wanted to do. Except sometimes he wanted to do it to a girl who was his girl. "Please just be quiet and then I won't have to hurt you." He tried to walk away from the schoolyard. He didn't want to have to move again. But he couldn't take his eyes from the children playing there. He watched their arms and legs move as they chased each other and saw one little girl stop to reach down and scratch herself. He wanted to talk to her. He wanted to take her clothes off and look at her. He wouldn't hurt her. He moved closer and stood quietly, watching. Which one? Which one would be the last to leave this time?

19.

In the morning, the front doorbell ringing awakened Tom. He rubbed his unshaven face and headed toward the door in his bare feet. When he reached the vestibule, he could see two policemen standing on the doorstep.

"Mr. N.," the taller of the two said. "May we come in?"

"Yes, of course," Tom said, leading the way back into the darkened hall. When he flicked the light switch inside his door, he turned again to face the dark uniforms. "What is it?" Had Alison been hurt in an accident? Was it Marilyn's plane?

"We understand you're the owner of the house. We'd like to ask some questions about the man who lives upstairs."

Tom was embarrassed by how little he knew as he found himself constantly saying, "I'm sorry, but I can't help you with that."

Squinty eyes, he thought. Brown? Blue? All he could tell them was the man's name (was it a false name?) and the colour and make of car he drove.

"Do you know how he makes his living, Mr. N.? Is he often away? What kind of hours does he keep?"

"Yes, he's often away."

"Have you seen him recently?"

Not often, but he had heard him. At that moment, the sound of the radio came through the floor from above and the two policemen looked at each other.

"Thank you, Mr. N."

Tom listened to them go up the stairs and to the shuffling noise as the tenant pushed back his chair to answer the knock on his door. Now he wanted only to be a dispassionate narrator...

20.

I know that as time passes I will sometimes forget the horrible sounds, the slightly sweet smell that filled my room, and the knowledge I might have saved her. But I can't stay here. I feel sorry for the landlord who was away that weekend and was as horrified as I was when the police found the body. Until this man, this monster, moved in, most of the tenants were students. But he didn't seem more than elusive until the events that shattered the neighbourhood. "He kept to himself," another tenant was quoted in the newspapers.

If they catch him somewhere, on a farm just below the border, in another rooming house in another city ... his name won't be the one on the social insurance card he gave at the factory. He will have shaved his beard. When he's arrested, he'll show the police the location of six other bodies, children who have been missing for months or even years. He'll be put in a maximum-security prison. Maybe he'll write and sell his memoirs. I don't believe in vengeance. But if he can do that, who can blame those who question the meaning of justice?

21.

Lynda stood at the doorway. "I'm hungry, Dad," she said.

"Let's go out to eat," Tom said, thinking of the greasy spoon restaurant at the corner with a sign in the window that advertised cheap breakfasts of eggs or pancakes and sausages between 8:00 and 10:30 a.m.

As they walked toward the door, there was a rumble of voices in the vestibule. The police stood with the man from the upstairs apartment between them. As they walked out and toward the street, Tom and Lynda watched them climb into a police car parked at the curb. One of the policemen remained on the sidewalk and beckoned to him.

"What's the matter, Dad?" Lynda whispered.

"I don't know," Tom said. He felt ill and didn't want to know. "Wait here for a moment, Angel." When he reached the curb, he stood with his fists clenched in his pockets, avoiding the eyes of the man in the cruiser.

"We'll want to talk to you later," the policeman said.

"Yes," Tom nodded.

"Dad," Lynda called as the car drove away.

"Um."

"I'm hungry."

"Okay, Angel," Tom said. "Just wait another moment, will you?" He walked toward the house again and stepped into the vestibule and up the stairs to find the door to his tenant's apartment stood half-open. He was about to close and lock it when his eyes fell on the guitar and he walked inside instead, noticing as he did that one guitar string was missing. There was a slight aroma of cologne that became stronger as he moved toward the bedroom. His hands began to tremble as he opened the door and surveyed the tangled sheets falling onto the floor. Words began to run unbidden through his mind once more ... *When I began to watch young women on the subway trains, I soon found I wanted to follow them when they stepped out of the car onto the platform. After a while, I realized I didn't know how they would react if I spoke to them so I followed them out of the station. There was always more I had to find out. How did very young girls respond to strangers? What did their bodies look like? I stood outside schoolyards and parks for weeks watching the children before I stopped one child. By then I had rented another room where I told them I did shift work so they wouldn't be suspicious when I rarely slept there. That was where I took most of the women I met in bars around the city. That was where the child was murdered ...* Tom backed away from the bedroom with tightly held breath. Had the man used a guitar string? What would he have done next if the police hadn't arrived that morning? *But even though I know enough now, I still watch the children in parks and schoolyards and notice young girls on the street. And I wonder why I watch this one rather than that one. Is it the way she smiles? The colour of her hair? The way she sits on the bus with the crotch of her underpants showing? Even if I knew, what can I do to stop myself? I wish the pounding in my head would disappear. It's like a hammer banging on my skull. Oh, please find me before there's another innocent body hidden in a garbage dump or a closet. Find me and stop me ...* Tom caught himself as he tripped on the edge of the carpet in the hall behind him.

"Dear God," he murmured.

As he wished the pounding in his head would disappear, he wondered what the police would surmise if he ever finished his story and they were to read it. Would they think they had the wrong man? Would a jury regard it as circumstantial evidence? Maybe he should give it up before he hurt someone. What if the story somehow hurt his own daughter? When he returned to find Lynda waiting for him, he couldn't look at her.

"Hello, Angel," he murmured.

"Let's go to eat, Dad," she said impatiently.

"Yes," he said. "Yes. Let's go to eat."

The Empty Chair

MARGARET WAS ALMOST NINETY and had been married sixty-four years when the train hit her husband. Reaching for his peaked hat, blown off when the subway came into the station, he fell against one of the cars.

Frank lay in a hospital bed with tubes inserted in his arm and an oxygen mask over his mouth and his nose. A clear plastic IV sack was attached to a pole beside his bed, and fluid ran slowly down through a tube into his arm. He was so weak he could scarcely move, and he whispered like a man with a bad case of laryngitis. For the entire two weeks he was in hospital, his head was clear enough to recognize Margaret, David, who was their only child, David's wife and his three grandchildren. And he was able to tell them what happened on the station platform.

Then he died.

Margaret couldn't go back to their Danforth Avenue apartment. From the living room, the city spread out before them. She'd become attached to the building, but she didn't even want to visit the place where she and Frank had lived for so long.

The apartment was full of mementos of their lives. Masks from Africa, Inuit sculpture, family photographs. The building itself was filled with the smells of the cuisine of countries from around the world and the sounds of a variety of languages.

Neighbours came to visit Margaret at her son's house in the Annex. They brought an assortment of food offerings: vegetable curries, pad thai, samosas, sweet and sour spare ribs. Every time Margaret saw a familiar face, she burst into tears.

"Mr. Frank was such a good man," someone would say.

Yes, although they couldn't have known how distant he could be at times. How preoccupied. Even so she missed him. She longed for the sound of his voice as he came in from one of his many meetings. Frank was an activist. He would say, "Someone has to go out and do it, Margaret. Storm the barricades." She remembered him marching in some protest or rally, like the one for housing alternatives for the homeless. And he chaired meetings: a committee on refugee issues, another on getting rid of nuclear weapons. But Frank had always been a peaceful man.

With her son's help, Margaret put her name down for an apartment in the seniors' complex she and Frank had talked about moving to. They had been on a waiting list, but whenever their names came up they decided to stay where they were.

It was a few months before an apartment was available. David designed the interior for her and moved in the things she wanted to keep. The sofa and chair she and Frank had bought recently. Her clothing. Photographs. Frank in his casual corduroys and shirt. Holding one of their grandchildren. The girl. What a treasure Katie was. The first grandchild. Now thirty. David was now in his late fifties. Scarcely a child any longer. But to her he was. She would protect him fiercely if anyone were to say something derogatory about him. But no one ever did. At least not that Margaret heard.

It was during her first week in the apartment that Margaret saw a man in the dining room at a table in the corner, tall, only slightly stooped, white hair, fine-rimmed glasses, sitting with three elderly women. Well, everyone there was elderly except the occasional guest, but she noted these three particularly because they were with one of two men in the dining room. It made her miss Frank across from her and, much to her surprise, she realized how much she longed for a man to sit with her.

One of the women had a gray bun with some yellow in it and another had a bald spot at the back of her head. He held court, the man did; she would tell David.

"Mother!" she could imagine him exclaiming, slightly shocked.

Margaret was finding it difficult to make friends in this seniors' building, something that surprised her. She'd never had that problem.

But sometimes she forgot what she'd been told and she could tell it irritated Thelma, who sometimes sat across from her at meals.

"I don't want to repeat myself every time we eat together," Thelma said at dinner. "Nor do I want to hear the same stories over and over."

Thelma didn't understand that Margaret's memory often failed her. "You know I had a concussion," Margaret said. It was true; she'd tripped one day three or four years ago walking on Danforth Avenue with Frank. She hit her head on the sidewalk and her left leg and shoulder were badly bruised. Fortunately, she didn't break anything.

And then she asked Thelma when the tea was. Each month, a day was set aside for everyone who had a birthday in it.

"I just told you," Thelma said.

"Oh, I'm so sorry," Margaret said. "And what was it you told me?"

Thelma sighed. "Thursday," she said. "Write it down."

They had both eaten chicken, although there were two other choices. Whenever it was chicken, Margaret ordered it. Some nights she cooked for herself upstairs in the blue kitchen. She called it that because Frank wasn't there to share it with her and it was actually painted a pale blue with darker laminate cupboards. Mostly if she ate in her apartment, she cooked food she bought in the huge supermarket on the main street to the south of the apartment. She knew where the deli counter was and she picked up salami and Black Forest ham there, salads, and bread. Ace bread, she liked the loaf with the dark olives in it.

She was surprised one evening when the man got up from his table and walked toward her. Margaret ate slowly and Thelma had already folded her white napkin, pulled out her walker and left.

"My name is Lawrence," the man said, peering down at her through his fine-rimmed glasses. The rims were almost black and his blue eyes were magnified. His delicate skin was scarcely lined, except between his eyebrows and across his forehead. What did he want?

"May I sit down?"

"Oh, yes," Margaret said. "Please do."

Of course, she didn't mind. She'd always wished to feel more comfortable with men. But she grew up in an era when guilt surrounded any feelings of attraction. This couldn't be anything but harmless. After all, she was almost ninety. And she didn't know how old he was, but he couldn't be much younger than that.

She never had an affair. And she regretted it. Not that there was anyone she'd wanted to have sex with. Not even Frank a lot of the time, for that matter. He was a cold man in many ways. Distant. No one knew because he was articulate and witty. And committed. It was a tribute, she thought, that they had survived sixty-four years together and in their later years had grown even closer.

Lawrence sat down in the chair across from her. "So," he said. "What's your name?"

"I'm sorry," she said. "Didn't I introduce myself? I'm Margaret."

"You're kind of classy, Margaret," he said.

Well, she hadn't expected such an old man to be a flirt. Classy? That could be true. She was tall and had always carried herself well, dressed well. It sounded like more than a compliment, but she wasn't versed in these things. Of course, she knew a lot, but her own experience was limited. She wondered if she should tell him about the concussion. What difference though would it make to him that she'd fallen to the pavement and hit her head, that her left leg had been bruised and scraped and her shoulder black and blue for ages? Frank had cared about that.

"Ohmygoodnessmargaret," her husband had said in one gush of breath and helped her to her feet. "We'dbettergetyoutoadoctor."

Lawrence leaned towards her on the other side of the table. "Something wrong?" he asked.

"No. No."

"My wife died," he said.

Margaret nodded. She could tell him about Frank, but she didn't want to. She understood that he was lonely and trying to make contact. But why her? He sat with three women.

"What did you say your name is?" she asked.

"Lawrence," he said.

"Oh yes. Do you live in one of the apartments, Lawrence?"

"Actually, I have a large room," he said. "With a big empty bed in it."

She thought he was handsome, but his eyes staring through the lens of his glasses made him look a little stupid. That was the most derogatory thing she could say about someone – being smart was something Frank had been. But this man was the kind about whom women would say, "One thing on his mind." Margaret thought all men were probably like that.

"I wondered," Lawrence said. "If I could visit you."

"Visit me?"

"Yes, in your apartment."

"Well," Margaret said. Maybe she should ask David. Imagine! Her son. He would think she was ridiculous. Imagining this man might want to make a pass at her. He'd likely fall over if he tried. "Maybe we could eat together first."

The next day they did. She asked him about his wife. A big woman, he told her. Not that tall, but big. He didn't use any other words. Not buxom or fat or round. Margaret could picture her with huge breasts that made her shoulders tired, held up by a bra that could hardly contain them. A black bra. Or a red one. No, likely a faded ivory one. And big bloomer-like panties under her sweatpants. Probably hadn't dressed up in later years, a white stripe down each leg of the sweatpants that she'd picked up at a Zeller's store. Cheap.

Lawrence had two daughters. One lived in San Francisco, the other off Danforth Avenue near a health food store. He knew about Greek town and all the restaurants on the Danforth that he didn't like to eat in because he liked meat and potatoes cooked the way he was used to. Like the big woman had cooked for him.

"The food here is okay," he said. "Not like at home, but at least they let you pick out something. They don't ram those foreign foods down your throat."

Frank was an engineer assigned to a project in Kenya. David, a young boy then, learned to speak Swahili. It hardly seemed possible that their son was now fifty-eight years old. Sometimes she had wondered how moving around would affect their son, but later she thought that he'd become the broad-minded person he was because of it.

"I like Indian and Chinese food," Margaret said. This was the third time they'd eaten together.

"Well, that's your problem," Lawrence said.

Margaret looked at him, what a stupid man he was. *Stupid. Stupid.* But she wanted him to sit with her. To just sit there. To be in that empty chair across from her.

"What about if I come to your place?" he said.

"When?"

"Tonight," he said.

"All right," she said. "I'll make tea."

"Tea?" He sounded irritated.

"Well, what do you want then?"

"I want to lie with you," he said.

Margaret pretended she didn't understand him. She stood and he followed her to the elevator. In the apartment, he sat on the sofa and fiddled with his hands, rather stocky hands covered with brown liver spots. Unlike her husband, she thought, Lawrence wasn't a well-educated man. No grasp of language or grammar. As a companion, likely boring. Frank was a delight with his pleasure in reading the classics and listening to music. It made up sometimes for the absences when he was at meetings. He was a complex mystery, full of challenges and surprises. How she missed him. Lawrence made her even more aware of what she'd lost.

"I'd like you to lie down with me," he said.

"I see." Although she didn't. "Where?"

"On your bed."

Margaret frowned. She'd never done anything like this. It might have made sense were she younger, but now! She was flustered, that was certain. Frank courted her when she was in her early twenties and he married a virgin. She didn't know how to handle this.

"Tell you what," he said. "You go in first and wait for me."

Margaret looked at a painting on the wall over his head. She wasn't sure this was what she wanted, although it was something she'd imagined trying for most of her adult life. There had been the time at a neighbourhood party when a man from across the street had suddenly kissed her lips in the kitchen and she'd recoiled in horror. But when she thought of it later, she'd liked the memory of the feel of someone other than Frank's lips on hers. She'd been too embarrassed to look at the man later, knowing she didn't want any more with him. He was too pushy. Did Lawrence contemplate sexual intercourse? Surely not. But it would be something to have tried it, wouldn't it? In her own bedroom in an apartment Frank had never seen. She would be betraying nothing. He's dead, she thought. After sixty-four years, he's dead. And she was lonely. So lonely.

Margaret put her cup down on the table beside her, sniffed into a white hanky, and stood up. She would walk into the bedroom and put on her silk pyjamas. She had one pair of pale blue slinky pyjamas. Just enough to satisfy fantasy most of the time.

She hung her clothes on a hanger in the closet and pulled on the long pants first, over legs that had become a sickly white colour with dark blue veins thrusting through the skin. Then she reached for the shirt with small buttons down the front. She fumbled with the buttons, her fingers getting tied up with each other. Like a silly schoolgirl, she thought. Maybe she would giggle. Her dressing gown was on the end of the bed and she pulled it over her chest so he couldn't see that the shirt buttons were open and her tired, old breasts hung down like pancakes above her slightly sagging belly. What a sad thing an old body was, she thought.

"Well?" Lawrence said impatiently, as he poked his head in the door. "Are you ready?"

Margaret sat up straight on the edge of the bed and looked at him. "How do I know you?" His face was familiar, but she couldn't remember his name or how they'd met. "Something to do with the dining room, wasn't it? Just remind me and then I'll know."

"We just ate dinner together," he said.

"Oh," she said. "So we did. Chicken."

"No, it was fish."

"Salmon."

"Some white stuff. I don't know what it's called."

"Sole maybe."

"Whatever you say, Margaret. Are you ready for me to lie down?"

Margaret looked at the robe she held tightly across her body like armour. Lawrence sat down next to her and pushed her gently over onto the bed. He pulled off the shirt that he had already unbuttoned and dropped it on the floor. Then he unzipped his trousers.

What's he doing? She could see a little penis with curly hair around it as he slipped out of his trousers and tugged at his underwear. He put his hand on her breast, pulled her gown open. He was breathing hard now. Her body was warm and she gasped as she felt him touch her pubic bone. She didn't want him to look at her, almost all the hair was gone as if she'd been shaved one day and nothing had grown back except a few scattered hairs. He pushed his hand lower and started to stroke her. What was he doing? Well, she knew, but was he crazy? She thought he'd just wanted to lie with her.

"Okay, Margaret," he said. "You're a real dish. Relax, will ya baby."

She wasn't sure what to do.

"Okay," he said again, this time gruffly. "Grab this, will ya baby?" He thrust himself toward her, took her hand and placed it on his small member. "Make it grow, baby," he said.

So she massaged his penis. And she twirled it around in her long fingers. So this was what she'd missed, she thought. It wasn't all that great after all. Just another penis. Grafted to a stupid mind. And this one didn't get any bigger.

"Christ," Lawrence said. "C'mon, baby. Make it grow."

C'mon, stupid, she thought. I'm doing the best I can. Twiddle it, fiddle with it, it doesn't grow.

After a while, he fell onto his back and stared at the ceiling.

"Shit," he said. "I can't get the bugger up."

So this was what she had longed for all her life, wondering what it would be like if some man besides Frank took an interest. And now here she was finally having succeeded, stuck with the hurt feelings of an old man who could no longer get an erection.

"It's all right, Lawrence," she said. "We can just lie here." She liked the feel of the warmth in her bed, cold for such a long time now.

He pushed himself up to a standing position and shuffled across the room with one pant leg on and the other off, like her son when he was a boy. He bent over to pick up his shirt and almost fell onto the carpet beside her.

"It's not all right," he said.

Margaret wrapped her gown tightly around her and followed him out to the foyer. When the door closed behind him, she put on the night latch, then walked to the kitchen.

"And that's that," she said aloud, reaching for a tea bag and plugging in the kettle.

The Golden Chain

TOWELS BRIMMED OVER THE edge of the basket Helen carried up the stairs from the basement, hiding the albatross on the front of her t-shirt. Tousled red hair, a hint of grey, still fell like flames to her shoulders. She started to sort the towels into piles – navy, purple, green – all dark colours. Sometimes she thought she might prefer the hassle that went with being with someone, although not the kind that went with being married again, than doing laundry alone on a Saturday night.

She thought the minor key of the music in the background – was it Schumann? – might be contributing to her mood. She decided to play some jazz instead. As the strains of Oscar Peterson at the piano swirled around her, she thought of dancing. Sometimes when she played music, she moved to the rhythm. She was going through her discs, picking one or two for later in the evening, when the telephone rang.

"Hello Helen."

Peter's deep voice sounded like truck wheels on heavy gravel. She always recognized it no matter how long it had been since the last time they spoke. He had intimated there wasn't much of a marriage and had seemed desperate as his kids gradually left home. But all he ever did about it was to work even harder for the big Bay Street law firm that swallowed him up for weeks and months at a time.

They met for lunch once or twice a year, fine menus with expensive food on white tablecloths. And aside from the golden chain he once gave her, that was the extent of their relationship. The gift had surprised her at the time. Even though she knew there were no strings, no obligations attached to it. When she opened the soft purple box, she held the chain so the sun shone on it as she let it glide through her fingers.

"Thank you," she said. "You shouldn't have, of course."

So while men came and went in her life, Peter was the one who had lasted. There was no affair, only the ongoing hint of something, the pleasure of ordering food together, of how he found her social causes and disdain at the corporate jungle a challenge rather than of no consequence. He never asked if there was a man in her life, although he surely must have figured out that often there must have been. So she expected him to say the usual: he was almost finished with some big deal and maybe they could do lunch in a week or two. But he had never called before on a Saturday night.

"Where are your kids?" he asked.

"They grew up and left home," she said, unable to resist the sardonic edge. "What's this about anyway?"

"I wondered if I could drop by."

"What?" Surprised, she couldn't think of anything else to say.

"So, may I?"

"All right."

Jeans and t-shirt seemed unlikely attire for a rendezvous with Peter, but Helen decided not to change. Only to comb her hair and put on a touch of lipstick. She recalled the postcard she once sent him from Amsterdam. *"I want to see you, touch you...."* It was as if it happened in another lifetime. She couldn't believe she'd ever been so impulsive. When she came home and he didn't call, she wanted to hide. Finally she wrote a letter to him about zoning – something like that – that was how they'd met after all, at meetings around the Spadina Expressway, at other meetings about a building near the corner of Bloor and Walmer. At the end of the letter, she said she would call him the following Tuesday.

"Funny," he said when she reached him. "I could scarcely see anything from the day I got your postcard until the day the letter came. The doctor said I had some kind of virus."

As soon as it cleared up, he went on working as hard as ever.

Amazing that this was ten years or so after the postcard and they had never talked about it, they just kept meeting for the occasional lunch. Except that night Peter arrived at her door half an hour later, carrying a bottle of wine in a brown paper bag. His hair was dishevelled and his face ruddy. As he followed her inside, he handed her the bag.

"Do you have wine glasses?"

"No. I gave them to Harry when we divorced and I never replaced them." She took out some parfait glasses from a cupboard above the kitchen sink. He leaned on the high counter between her and the dining room.

"My wife's skiing," he said.

"Don't you ski?"

"No."

Watercolours were arranged on the counter where Helen had left them earlier after painting a few strokes of a cliff that jutted out into the ocean. Grey clouds with dabs of navy, purple, green, and yellow almost filled the sky.

"I didn't know you painted."

"On weekends."

Helen could tell he didn't like the painting by the way he clenched his jaw and looked past it to the window.

"I usually watch the hockey game on Saturday nights," he said as he surveyed the room, his eyes lingering on the framed Picasso poster over the microwave.

"If you want to know the score, the television is in the living room," she said.

His face lit up. "Are you coming?"

"No. But feel free."

"Well, I'll just check." He took his glass and she heard his footsteps go into the front room and cross the floor to the sofa.

She suddenly slashed black paint across the cliff and the sky. Then she stared at the painting until Peter came back into the kitchen. All the years it had taken to reach this moment loomed up between them. Why the moment was now made no sense to her.

"Why did you do that?" he asked.

"I felt like it."

"I liked it."

"Who's playing?" she asked.

"You mean you really don't know?" He sounded astounded.

"No."

"The Leafs and Pittsburgh."

"Is it a good game?"

"Yes. But I came to see you, not the hockey game."

Helen noticed that he had deep, dark circles under his eyes and the skin on his face had become lined and puffy.

"I dream about you," he said. "And when I wake up at four or five in the morning, I get up and drive around. For the last two months, I've often driven by your house in the middle of the night." He spoke in a jumble of sentences that all ran together, sentences that didn't make any clearer to her why he was here now rather than at any other time in the last ten years. Maybe his wife was about to leave him. It would have to be something quite unusual or dramatic. She thought of his sleek grey Oldsmobile driving along downtown streets, past her door, in the darkness of the graveyard shift. Maybe one of the nights when she was pacing the floor herself.

"I saw a light one night. I thought maybe you had it on a timer."

"Some are." She didn't say she dreamed about him. She knew there was nowhere to go with him, nowhere at all. If he hadn't had that virus, there might have been. She believed it was just a name some doctor gave his condition because he couldn't explain his partial blindness. In her heart, she knew that it was her postcard.

"I had tests at the hospital last week," he said.

"What kind of tests?"

"CAT scan." He'd blacked out at a meeting. It also happened twice a year earlier. The results of all the tests then had come back clear.

"And your wife's skiing?"

"Yes."

"Come on, Peter. You say it as if that's where she should be. Why are you really here?"

"I don't want to die," he said. "I have a friend who dropped dead of a heart attack last month. That's what lawyers do. Die in their fifties. I'm sorry. I shouldn't be going on like this. But I put everything on hold and now there isn't going to be time for most of it. Maybe not for any of it."

"Why don't we watch the hockey game?"

"Okay."

He piled pillows behind his head as he stretched out on the sofa, leaving room for her beside him. She leaned back and let her head nestle in the crook of his arm. She felt strangely disconnected from everything.

"I really don't care about hockey," he said as he touched her breast through her t-shirt. She murmured as he put his hand under her bra and fingered her nipple.

"I shouldn't do this." He stared at the ceiling. "This is bizarre."

"Why?"

"I've wanted this for years, but I never thought it would happen."

She didn't need a map to know she was up against another dead end. But she couldn't ignore that whether or not she ever saw him again, this was something they both still wanted.

After a while, locked in each other's arms, moving to the rhythm which mounted between them, she thought he was shaped a little like a small, wooden figure someone had brought her from Russia once, all round at the middle and tapering off at the head and feet. Funny how that wasn't how he looked in clothes at all, more like all the men on the subway with their masks carefully in place, not suddenly moaning and flailing as he'd begun to do. The whole sofa was rocking. Maybe the whole house. And as she felt the clenching and letting go in the walls of her vagina, making sounds she didn't even try to stifle, she started to laugh. And when he let go in one burst of sound, she lay back, her hands behind her head.

"You're a bit of a tiger," she said.

"I feel wonderful," he said. "It's like a miracle. I thought I'd forgotten how. You're going to think I'm crazy, but it's like riding a bicycle."

She turned her head slightly to look at him.

"I haven't told anyone yet," he said. "There's a tumour behind my right eye. The neurologist called me this morning."

"What?" she said. "Oh my God." He should have told her before he came. He should have let her decide what she wanted. She thought of the black streak through her painting and imagined putting another across it in the other direction.

"I won't be able to say anything at the office," he said. "It's a cut-throat business. If I do, they'll be lining up for my job."

"What?" she repeated. How could he be talking about the office now?

"That's the way large firms are," he said. "There's always someone ready to pounce if you show any signs of weakness."

"I didn't say I didn't believe you."

Peter watched her put on her jeans and the t-shirt with the albatross on it. "He said he'd tell me more Monday," he said. "The neurologist. But I'm not supposed to drive." Then he added, "It's inoperable."

She reached across and took both his hands. "Just be quiet for a while, Peter," she said. "Just be quiet. Let's just sit and be quiet. We'll talk in a while."

"I feel awful about tonight," he said. "Will you forgive me?"

"There's nothing to forgive."

"So, are we still friends?"

"Come on. What a question."

After a while, he looked at his watch. He appeared calmer. "I have to go home now. On Monday I'll see the doctor to find out more. He said something about chemotherapy."

"Why don't you stay the night?"

"I don't know why I waited so long," he said. "I always wanted you. Now it's too late. I'm going to die. I don't want to die." He followed her upstairs, stretched out on her bed and let her hold him.

Helen was quiet. All those wasted years they might have had together. All those wasted years when she thought he might do something dramatic. Like figuring out what he wanted and taking the plunge. It was the nature of his work that fooled her, she thought, full of risk and high drama. But in his own life, he was paralyzed.

In the morning, he stood awkwardly in the hallway as she buttoned the middle of his coat and hugged him gently. As they walked to the door, he kept touching the side of his head. "I didn't even feel anything before," he said. "Now it's as if there's a great big ball there."

"Did you notice who won the hockey game?" she asked.

"You must be kidding."

"No," she said. "I figured you'd have noticed."

"When?"

"I don't know." She shrugged.

He didn't answer, but on the porch he raised his fingers to his lips.

"Thanks," he said.

That night she dreamed of driving a large van and stopping to crack eggs on the street. When she attempted to gather up the eggs, bits of dirt stuck to them. She realized she should hurry – after all, who prepared food in the middle of University Avenue? So she drove quickly away, but she couldn't keep the van on the road – ran over curbs, up onto flowers, jumped lanes, and finally got back into the right lane only when a police car passed her. She was sure she'd be stopped then, but the car didn't even flash its lights. She woke up.

"You bastard," she whispered.

Glasses, two long-stemmed, arrived at Helen's door in a parcel from Ashley's the next week. On the card, he'd written, "*The Leafs won.*"

Light gleamed through one of the glasses as she held it up to the beam from the chandelier over the dining room table. She considered throwing it into the fireplace where it would smash on the brick and fall into the ashes of the last fire.

She began to shudder and she could feel her hands and lips trembling. She could spend the months ahead, between now and the next time she lit the fireplace, reading obituaries. But she wasn't going to do that. She'd start to go out on Saturday nights.

Months later, Peter called as if nothing had happened. They had lunch in a restaurant on Queen Street not far from the lake. A Greek restaurant with the windows opened to the street. Young girls walked by in bright shorts and tops. Men put their arms around them or stood on the pavement and watched. Peter looked fine to her, although he said he was still having treatments. Afterwards they walked down to the beach where they stood and watched white-crested waves rise in the wind.

"What do you see?" he asked.

"I'm listening to the wind," she said. "I'm watching the waves dance." What the hell did he expect her to say?

"I'll be out of town for a while," he said. "As soon as the chemo is finished. I'll call you when I get back."

"Whatever."

Dancing had become her passion. The salsa, the rhumba, swing, she danced them all. She wasn't going to dance alone any more. Or sort towels ever again on Saturday night. For all she knew, Peter might still be driving by on her street in the middle of the night, but she never looked out to see if she might catch sight of him. A few weeks later, she found a message on her machine, "Thanks for lunch."

It was a long time before she ran into him. It was at a fundraiser for a local politician. Peter greeted her cheerfully. Other than noticing that his hair was a little thinner, he didn't seem much different. He said he had been in France for two months. "We went to Paris and Nice and to castles and vineyards on the Rhone," he said. "We tasted wine and walked on the pebbly beaches of the Mediterranean."

"What about you?" he asked. "What are you up to? Are you still living in the same house? Still painting?"

"Yes." She didn't ask him what happened to the tumour. She didn't want to hear that it was some kind of virus.

"You know that card you sent me from Amsterdam…" he began to say, his eyes meeting hers.

Her neck reddened and the flush spread up to her face. The ice in her glass made a tinkling sound.

"I remember ice forming on the wings of the plane at Schipol Airport," she said. "And the large duty-free shop there. I bought a watch. And a bottle of wine. I rode a bicycle around Amsterdam with a young man I met in a restaurant. It was his girlfriend's bike. I ate with both of them, but she'd gone to Portugal by the time we got around to riding. To the Algarve."

"You didn't tell me any of that."

She'd stayed in a small room high up over a canal. To get to it, she had to walk up four or five flights of stairs. Swans glided across the water below her as she sat at her window. She looked down at their white shapes and at bicycles on the street. And wrote the words in her head dozens of times before she finally bought the card.

"Any of it," Peter repeated. "You didn't tell me."

"I guess I didn't."

"I should have asked," he said.

"I went to see one painting in the Rijksmuseum," she said, not responding to him, not saying the obvious. "Only one. Rembrandt's 'Night Watch.' And after I stood and looked at it from every conceivable angle, I walked out onto the street again. I went to see Edvard Munch's 'Scream' in Oslo a few years later also. Just that one painting."

"My postcard is a Van Gogh," he said.

"Ships," Helen said, recalling the bright colours that had drawn her to that painting. A red hull, a yellow one. On a beach. It was in Amsterdam that she'd lost the gold chain Peter had given her. She had looked everywhere for it. When she left, the owner of the hotel wrote her address in a small book so he could contact her if anyone found it, but she never heard anything. Later she discovered that the hotel's name, *Le Gouden Ketting*, was Dutch for the golden chain.

"I still have it," he said.

A Country Weekend

BERT MAINVILLE STOOD AT the screened window of the balcony that overlooked the lake. Two birches at the edge of the water met in an arch overhead. Stumps marked the spots where years ago he had cleared away the trees so that now he could see pine stretching off into the distance and growing from cliffs of rock on the opposite shore. From a cloud bank moving slowly across the far sky a jagged streak of lightening hung momentarily suspended. But the sun continued to stream down on the water and the dark clouds moved slowly away to the east.

Bert continued to stare at the water. In the cabin behind him he could hear the women chattering and laughing a little as they unpacked the boxes they had brought north from the city. North on the wide divided highway to Barrie, through fields of open farmland, onto another highway, undivided, that began to meet more pine trees and the ski hills, bare swaths down through the pine in summer. Then onto yet another highway that had in places been blasted through sheer rock and emerged suddenly to overlook a glistening lake or river, some with boats lined up at docks near the road. North finally to the dirt road that lead down to the Mainville cottage at Bear Point where Bert had to drive carefully to avoid the rocks which on occasion scraped the undercarriage of the car. He drew in large breaths of air gratefully, noting almost automatically that there was no pain in his chest this time but feeling nonetheless for the small bottle of nitro-glycerine tablets to make sure they were there before he could listen to the contrasting sounds of the north, sounds he always thought of as the sounds of silence after the city. Some were loud, but with a certain soothing rhythm, the waves on the shore below, the wind rustling in the leaves, the cry of the loon, birds chirping. He had become used to the occasional rumbling of cars and trucks on the highway at the end of the bay, scarcely heard it at all any more.

In the kitchen, Thelma Mainville opened the refrigerator door and put fresh fruit and vegetables into a tin tray on the bottom shelf – a bunch of green, seedless grapes and a firm honeydew melon, carrots and wax beans – while her older sister, Grace, stacked tins in the cupboard.

"Did you bring flour, Thelma?" Grace asked.

"No."

"I thought I might bake a cake."

"Just relax, Grace," Thelma said. "We don't often bake here."

"I like to cook. I've always liked to cook," Grace said and looked dreamily out the window. "I've been thinking I'd like to set up a little tea shop at Niagara-on-the-Lake. With tea and sandwiches. But you know, those special little sandwiches with a certain flair, a certain touch. I could make a fortune."

Thelma sighed and said nothing. She had almost forgotten Grace's pipe dreams, the endless daydreams she weaved aloud, never considering any of the practical aspects, never putting them to the test. Even at seventy. She continued putting the food away in silence.

"Are there beds to be made, Thelma?" Grace asked after a while.

"Why, thank you, Grace," Thelma said, directing her sister to the box with the sheets and pillowcases. As she walked across the living room toward the bedrooms with her, Thelma could see Bert without really turning to look at him, a grey-haired man looking out over the water ... *has always done that, gone right to the window ...* and she also heard voices now, unfamiliar voices, young ones, echoing up from the water, from the cottage next to them ... *you, too, Bert, what dream, what regret, what memory? ... Still, you've worked hard, not built pies in the sky.*

"It must be five years since I last saw you," Grace said.

"At least," Thelma said. "It doesn't feel that long though."

"Do you remember Grandfather Boyd, Thelma?" Grace asked.

"Yes," Thelma said, laughing suddenly.

"The porch," Grace said. "Do you remember the tall tales he always told on the porch? With everybody laughing."

"Everybody but Grandmother," Thelma murmured, but Grace did not hear her.

"And as the evening wore on, the liquor flowed, and all the children, the little ones, were quickly taken away. Put to bed somewhere where the sounds were muffled."

And we wondered, Thelma thought, wondered what else was going on, always a little frightened at a sudden loud noise and later the groping noises of adults finding their way to their beds, of …

"I used to creep down and listen," Grace said.

"I remember his horses," Thelma said. "A beautiful stallion … and the candy before the races."

"What a mad Irishman. Always going to have the best race horse in the county," Grace laughed.

"Yes," Thelma said, suddenly tired. "But he never did, did he?" *Do you wonder always if this is the last time now, Bert? Are you frightened? A proud, restless man, still cuts his grey hair in a brush cut as if he were thirty years younger … if he were thirty years, no forty years, maybe more, younger, he'd be wearing it long … oh, Bert … Does Grace remind you because she's here, because Ned died, or is it another young family in the Belmont's cottage?* At the end of the day, he would make his usual diary entry, a ritual he had performed for thirty years, but even if she saw it, it would reveal nothing, would be just another short, repetitive entry. Precise and clipped. Never mentioning his work, all the meetings, endless days and nights of meetings. Only the weather. Brief comments about their daughter, Ginny. Thelma had come across the diary once (he had made no attempt to conceal it or even keep it closed, on several occasions had shown her an entry or two … to tell her it had rained the morning before Ginny's wedding, when their grandson's tonsils had come out, how big the fish was he had caught on a certain Sunday twenty-five years ago), but she had learned nothing. Nothing about how he felt about anything, why he kept notes on all the trivia of a lifetime, but nothing about why before Ginny had begun to grow up he had needed his "women,"

about how he felt about the heart attack. At most there was sometimes a baffling phrase included, but even that was rare. Today's entry
would probably read ... "Bear Point. July 25. Sky clear. Sun. Temp.
75 degrees. Began to read book on...? Gift from Ginny (or Thelma,
or borrowed from library July 24). Grace for weekend. New people
in Belmont cottage." Rarely more than that. Usually less.

"Oh, but that wasn't important," Grace said.

"I think it was to him," Thelma said, remembering again the
whisky bottles after the races, the loud voices, being whisked away
by her mother or her grandmother. At least that had been different
with Bert. What he struggled with he did not make noise about.
She hated noise.

Their voices trickled out onto the porch, but Bert did not hear
what they were saying. The two of them together were like a self-
contained unit, a phalanx, and on the way up in the hot, dusty car
he had wondered sporadically what he was doing even though he
knew that as many weekends as possible he had always had to escape. From the city. Even though he loved it. From the unalleviated
activity of the whole apparatus of government. Although he thrived
on it. To be somewhere else. To read books, not the endless array
of requests for reports and the technical reports which constantly
covered his desk. It went on forever ... *Mr. B. Mainville, Commissioner of Transportation, has been requested to have his staff prepare*
... the pile of requests growing like a pile of garbage in that dump
down the road while he sat at meetings, answering questions in one
breath and signing correspondence which should have been looked
after days ago in between. This time he had a book on the Pelopen-
nesian war tucked in with his shaving gear and pyjamas. Thelma
sometimes said he devoured history. But it was more accurate to say
it devoured him. When he read he became so absorbed that he often
felt he was living in the time and events he was reading about. In
the course of history, its vast panorama, the relative insignificance
of everything that was annoying him fell briefly into perspective.
Then he could return and face another round of questioning from
the elected representatives at committees, of public meetings when

he was there in the background, ready to be called at any point to respond to a technical question, to explain ... *Ladies and gentlemen, our Commissioner will respond to that if you will be so kind as to ...*

But usually he and Thelma came alone. Or with one of the grandchildren. Now he felt surrounded by the clucking of women, greyhaired women with blue and purple veins in their white, mottled legs, sagging breasts, the brown mole on Grace's cheek with spiky grey hairs mixed still with some darker ones that had become less prominent with age. He dreaded seeing their bodies, sagging in all the wrong places, multitudes of fat pockets, swimming down there off the dock. But, after all, it was Thelma's weekend, he reminded himself. She had spent so many hours by his bed in the hospital after the heart attack, been so patient when he came home ... *but that woman has to stop treating me like a bloody invalid...* Suddenly Bert clenched his fist with an intense longing to smash the screen.

"Can I get you anything before we make the beds, dear?" Thelma called.

"Uh ... oh, no thanks ... I think I'll just go down and look at the boat."

"All right, dear. Be careful though."

Bert grimaced and pushed open the screen door, walked toward the dock where the boat was moored. It was still carefully covered with the canvas top as he had left it the previous Sunday before they left. He undid the hooks on the canvas and shook off the water that had accumulated in the crevices before rolling it back and folding it. He heard voices down the lake and looked toward the next dock where a man and a boy were standing on the end of it, fishing. For a while he watched them wistfully, then put the canvas he was still holding away in the small shed at the edge of the water.

Above, in the cabin, Thelma stood at the bedroom door. "I think everything you need is in that box," she said.

"You know, I'd give anything to have a little bungalow of my own," Grace said abstractedly.

"Um," Thelma said. "Well, I hope you know you're welcome here any time, Grace."

"When I stopped dancing the teacher said 'If you set up a school, stay out of my territory,'" Grace laughed. "Why, if I'd started a dancing school I could have made a fortune. Look at Arthur Murray. And I'd have my bungalow."

Thelma retreated quietly, looking down at the water where she could see Bert on the dock, could tell he was watching the people on the next one. And she felt unaccountably resentful and angry, couldn't smile at the thought of his nostalgia, his hankering. Since his illness, and since Ned died, she couldn't stifle the memories that evoked more and more muffled anger. She straightened the cloth on the small round table where they ate their meals, thoughts pouring in, all the dance floors in the early days when she was lucky to have one dance with Bert, all the times she felt awkward and uncomfortable while he jauntily entertained one person after another. Once, as she sat at the table with someone while Bert whirled another woman around the floor, his words wafted back to her. "Oh, yes. Well, of course, Thelma's quite phlegmatic...." *Phlegmatic? Because I was always there waiting when you came down, Bert?* ... Thelma could feel the anger gush up, and then ebb ... *what's the use?* ... She had loved Grandfather Boyd more than anyone other than Bert ... *maybe I needed the stars ... and he always came back.* They had never spoken angry words to each other then. She had seen the women as only a way of proving himself to himself. And she could not bear the thought of people arguing, quarrelling, of muffled, angry sounds in the night. It was easier to pretend she had not seen, to ignore ... but it was becoming more difficult now. Ever since the gripping pain in his chest and the gasping for breath, since the resuscitation and the careening trip in the ambulance, the protracted intensive care in the hospital. What testing ground that would not kill him could convince him now that he was still strong, as strong as he had never believed he was even when he still was. Thelma felt she had to watch him, to protect him or she might really lose him. She leaned on the window frame, wiping sudden tears from her eyes, pulling herself painfully together ... *quiet, competent Thelma?* ... patting her hair into place, sighing one last long sigh.

Bert looked down and saw the sun gleaming on the tails of min-
nows darting after flies on the surface of the water directly in front
of him. He kneeled to untie the boat, to pull it around to the ladder
and climb down into it. Then he shoved it gently away from the
dock with an oar and before rowing it, checked the fuel gauge on the
gas tank. Gripping the oars skilfully, he manoeuvred the boat until
the bow was heading down the lake, and started then to cut a small
swath in the water as he moved slowly away from the dock. Not in
a mad dash of spray as he had as a young man, but lingering along
the shoreline, watching the people, inspecting the cottages from the
water to determine which ones were occupied, day dreaming ... *last
night I had a dream, I dreamed I swam the lake* ... Bert's brow fur-
rowed as the dream came back to him and he looked across the bay
remembering that a few years earlier he could still swim the lake ...
today I am too tired ...

A red canoe slipped out from the shore propelled forward by the
slim hands of a young woman ... *like Ginny* ... *about thirty, pretty,
slim* ... *but what does she know?* ... the paddle dipping into the mirror smoothness of the water, glistening beads of water falling from
it as it lifted, moved forward, then plunged deep again, silently, the
lone canoe gliding forward along the shore in the opposite direction
toward the rocky point in the distance.

Bert watched the canoe slip away ... *I swam this lake* ... *listen to
me, for Chrissake, listen, I swam this lake* ... *and I took all the fucking
shit, thirty years of changing waves of politicians, changing vogues* ...
"*Oh, Bert, you accomplished so much,*" *Thelma's voice as he lay in the
hospital.* "*What? WHAT?*" *he demanded then, almost shouting.* "*Calm
down, dear. Calm down,*" *she remonstrated softly.* "*Think of the roads
that weren't there or even dreamed of thirty years ago ...*" "*What a perfect
wife for someone with so much drive, so much ambition.*" *How many
times has someone or other said that?* ... "*AW SHUT UP.*" *Roads aren't in
vogue any more, and none of them is called the Mainville Throughway
or even Mainville Street* ... *the hurt look, never shouted at her before,
ever...* "*Thelma, I'm sorry. I'm sorry.*" ... *Sorry for saying shut up or sorry
I never shouted before or sorry for forgetting to remember something I*

really don't even know ... The oars began to slip out of his hands and Bert caught them with a sudden grabbing motion and sat holding them with his lips compressed, finally removed them one at a time, shook the water gently off, and laid them separately along the inside edge of the boat. Then he moved carefully to the back of the boat, pulled the cord that started the engine. It began to sputter almost at once, so Bert turned to the lever and jiggled with it until some connection caught again and the engine ran smoothly. He brought the bow around to face the cabin and moved slowly toward the dock. Grace was swimming and as he turned the motor off to glide in the last few feet he watched her flowered bathing cap bob around in the water. She did not really swim any more, but moved around slowly in a jerky pantomime. The flowered cap bobbed toward the ladder and he watched Grace's blue-veined legs as she climbed up onto the dock, hastily picking up a lilac terry-cloth robe and encircling her white, goose-pimpled flesh. Hot sweat began to form all over his body and a tight, dry knot to gather in his throat.

"Are you going to swim, Bert?" Grace called.

"Yes," he said. "I'm going to swim the bay."

Neither Grace nor Bert saw Thelma walking toward them. But Thelma caught Bert's words and, with a worried frown, turned and moved quietly back to the cabin. Grace sat down in a large wooden chair and watched Bert as he tied the boat to its moorings.

"Bert," Thelma called from above after a few moments. "Bert!"

He looked up toward the balcony. Thelma beckoned to him. He sighed and walked slowly across the mossy surface to the door. Small toads jumped from their hiding places under the roots as his heavy steps descended and he brushed away a mosquito circling near his ear with a sweeping motion of his right arm.

"Hello. Like a cool drink? A gin and tonic maybe?" Thelma asked gaily. "And what were you doing?"

"No, thanks ... Yes. As a matter of fact, I think I will. But orange juice, a big glass of orange juice ... I was just getting the boat ready," Bert said, annoyed slightly at how she always had to probe. For a woman who had wanted to keep their lives private, as separate from his career as possible, he often wondered how she could know so little of the sanctity of the minutiae of personal privacy. Sometimes she was like a child.

"Orange juice," Thelma repeated, lines of puzzlement in her forehead.

"Yes, orange juice," he said.

"All right."

He stood in the doorway watching Thelma disappear into the kitchen, watching her hips which had thickened and the gnarled veins which showed at the backs of her knees just below the hem of her dress, and her white hair cut short and curled gently in a permanent wave, the bluing a little more prominent than usual. Still, with all the lines in her face, with the skin that had become leathery on her neck, he thought that she was still a good-looking woman.

"Are we going to play cards, Bert?" Grace asked, startling him because he hadn't heard her come quietly up behind him. She walked onto the porch and sat under the window of the living room with her beach robe around her, holding her hands knotted in her lap.

"That's a good idea," Bert said. "But not now. Tonight." And then, "It's been a long time since we played cards together, Grace."

"Umhm. The last time was over five years ago. Bridge ... with Ned. Do you remember?"

"Yes," Bert said quietly, remembering Ned, big, reliable Ned. He looked away obliquely with a sudden catch in his throat and a new wave of hot sweat all over his body.

Thelma stood in the doorway again, looked back and forth between the two of them, said nothing. She handed Bert the glass of orange juice she was holding, a glass with his fraternity crest on it, but he did not notice.

"In about half an hour, I'm going to swim the lake, Thelma. You can come in the boat. Like we used to do for Ginny. Although she never had any trouble ... not even the first time," he said, a small, proud smile creeping into his eyes and his voice.

Grace got up quietly, walked between the two of them, holding herself so that she felt as small, as inconspicuous as possible and crossed the living room to the smaller of the two bedrooms and closed the door gently behind her. A towel hung from a hook on the wall behind the door and she reached for it, stood with one foot at a time over the wastebasket and began to brush dry grains of sand from her ankles and between her toes.

"What are you trying to prove, Bert?" Thelma asked.

"It's just a ten minute swim, Thelma. Probably less than a quarter of a mile. It's no big deal."

"Bert. You don't need to, you know."

"You'll have to change, Thelma," Bert said and turned and walked into their room where he set the orange juice down on the dark, scratched top of the dresser and began to rummage through the drawers, looking for a bathing suit.

Thelma stood listening to the sounds inside, to the drawers opening and closing, wondering if there was any way she could stop him. She looked out over the water with a deep frown, tapping her fingers nervously on the window sill, remembering the first time Ginny swam the lake, when all they had was a tent because that was the year they'd built the cabin. And a grey, flat-bottomed boat. And she had rowed then, too. Bert sat in the back never taking his eyes from Ginny. "You're doing fine," if she looked up while she swum playfully, laughing at the sound a distant motor made under the water. She swivelled from her back quickly then, bobbed, and looked at them. "What a funny sound it makes underwater," she laughed, her red, wet hair streaming straight around her shoulders, her voice echoing and reverberating through the air. "You're doing fine," Bert had said, wooden with concentration, almost as if that concentration would keep her afloat. And Thelma had felt constantly on the verge of vomiting. But they'd reached the other side where Ginny had climbed sylph-like from the water, still laughing as she stood on the rocks waiting for them. Bert had turned to Thelma. "I'll row back," he had said tersely.

"No, I'll row," she snapped.

But when Ginny was in the boat, wrapped in a towel, the knots in Thelma's head, her throat, her muscles had begun to ease and when they reached shore she had gone to make hot chocolate for all of them while Bert and Ginny pulled the boat up onto the shore and tied it to a tree.

"You're not ready," Bert said and Thelma jumped.

"No."

"Well, I'll go down and wait at the boat."

He went out, letting the screen door slam behind him.

Thelma walked slowly to their room. An old pair of faded blue dungarees hung on a hook, left there week after week. Like another character she played, Thelma thought as she hung her dress on a hangar in the small closet and tugged on the faded pants slowly. Then she pulled out the first shirt she came to, an old checked one of Bert's, and put it on, turning quickly away from her image in the clouded surface of the mirror. She thought of lying down on the bed and just resting, falling asleep, but was apprehensive that then Bert might just go ahead and swim anyway. And if he got tired in the middle of the lake ... well ...

Still, as she sat on the edge of the bed, an old double bed that had begun to sag in the middle ... *but if he gets tired ...*

Bert was standing on the dock holding the rope that was attached to the boat.

"Well," Thelma said. "Here I am."

"I'll get the motor running for you," Bert said.

"I'd rather row."

"You don't need to."

"No. But I don't like that motor. And I can't hear anything when it's running anyway."

"All right then. When you get out a few yards I'll start to swim after you. Head for that point," Bert said, pointing in the direction of the shortest distance across. "And try not to get too far away from me."

"Yes," she sighed. "Yes, I remember all that."

"It's calm now so you shouldn't have much trouble."

Thelma held the side of the boat and started to get in. Bert reached out and held her arm to steady her. As she moved out into the lake the boat jerked awkwardly. She tested her strokes with one oar, then the other, before taking a few steady strokes to a point beyond his depth, heading toward the opposite shore. She sat with the oars motionless then, waiting, while Bert climbed part way down the ladder and holding on with one hand splashed water onto his arms, his face, his chest, before diving in. He swam at first with a slow, easy stroke, feeling the boat begin to move away from him as he approached it. When he felt a little tired he rolled over onto his back, swimming slowly with his arms and legs moving in a gentle, relaxed rhythm, watching the shore recede gradually behind him and the blue sky above the trees. After a while, a gust of wind, turning quickly to a mere breeze, rippled the water around him, moving him slightly sideways so that he had momentarily to work harder to keep going. He turned to see if he was on course with the boat and noticed it was a little further away than it had been when he turned onto his back.

"Try to stay closer," Bert shouted. He swam on his side, but the breeze had become a little stronger, a steady series of waves forcing him ever so slightly away from the path he felt he was attempting to follow. He looked at the boat again and it was even farther away now.

"Am I heading the right way?" he shouted.

There was no answer, but he saw Thelma look toward the shore, then at him, and turn the boat one way, then the other, before straightening it out again. So he began to swim slowly toward it, vaguely tired all over. He wondered how deep the water was and for the first time he felt a little frightened.

"Get closer now," he yelled at Thelma with as much strength as he could muster. And angrily because he felt that she could if she really wanted to. His breathing became heavier and more difficult with each stroke.

Thelma struggled to stay close to him and to keep heading toward the rocky shore at the closest point, but just as she seemed to have the boat heading in the direction she wanted small gusts of wind that seemed to blow up unexpectedly from some unseen centre kept forcing it to float away slightly. She felt as if the boat, and Bert swimming after it, were zigzagging across the lake, tacking helplessly with the wind rather than following the shortest distance between two points and she was close to tears ... *refuse to do anything like this again, Bert. If you want to kill yourself, you can kill yourself without my help* ...

"Am I on course?" Bert shouted, his voice high with frustration, fatigue, and anger. He felt as if they were going around in circles. Thelma, this is the last time, he thought. And for a moment he felt peaceful. Until he looked at the boat and knew that if he had to he could no longer reach it and that Thelma wouldn't have the strength to save him.

"I don't know," Thelma called desperately.

Bert's head pounded and his lungs ached. He felt dizzy. "FOR CHRIS-SAKE, DO YOU FUCKING WELL WANT ME TO DROWN?" he shouted in a loud echoing voice that took all his remaining strength. He saw the hurt look crowd out Thelma's features just as he started to roll onto his back again but he just laid there, scarcely moving, too tired to think of anything but the pounding of his heart against his ribs, the sudden slight pain which had begun in his back whenever he propelled himself forward with a strong knifelike kick.

Thelma watched his grey head in the water with swirling anger invading her, drying up the tears and the lump in her throat. She hated him, wanted suddenly to bash his head with the oar, to see him sink under the water, to see the lake close over him until nothing remained. Nothing...

She heard the sound of a motor in the distance and turned, apprehensive, to see where it was coming from. It was a long way off and heading away from them. She watched the wide gully it left in the water behind it, knowing that the waves when they reached her wouldn't add to the breezes buffeting the old rowboat Bert was following across the water.

Thelma watched the big boat disappear, imagining that she would turn to watch Bert again and that he wouldn't be there. That she wouldn't see him anywhere. Bert, she thought, with sudden panic.

Bert. She turned to scan the water, and there WAS no sign of him anywhere. For a moment, she thought she saw him then, but when she began to head toward the white spot on the water a gull rose into the air. Bert, she thought. Bert. Oh my God, Bert. What have I done? She stood up and the boat rocked precariously, but still she could see only water.

"BERT!" she screamed. "BERT!"

A weak voice reached her then. "Thelma. Thelma. Over here."

And she could feel her breath go out in a long sigh of relief and tears gathering in her eyes as she saw him approaching her very slowly. She sat down and brushed away the tears, reaching for the oars again, letting him swim slowly, slowly toward the boat and when he waved her weakly aside, toward the rocks that were so close now. So close now.

Dazed, tired beyond recall, Bert knew that if he reached the opposite shore he would never swim the lake again, but all he wanted now was to get there. It had really occurred, he thought. Even after the heart attack, the hospital, the constant need for nitro-glycerine, still he had often been encompassed with bewildered disbelief. Or anger he was too tired for now. Disbelief and anger that Bert Mainville was just an ordinary man who'd had a heart attack, an old man who could putter around the lake in his boat, but that a swim across the bay really belonged to a memory. Or a dream…

Finally he did climb shakily from the water onto the rocks, breathing so heavily that each time it sounded as if he was gasping for his last breath. And for a long time he just stood there, partially hunched over, holding himself with his arms.

Thelma sat in the boat just off shore, eased in gradually closer to the rocks. He looked at her, still huddled over. But she avoided his eyes at first. Then looked at him, relief evident in her face, around all the lines of her eyes and mouth, but a paroxysm of undissolved fear still in her stomach, knowing now in a different way than she had by the hospital bed that he was going to die. No, not today. But that it would happen. And that she would never be ready. But that there was no way of taking that into account. How could anybody ever be ready? Even if she had been a different kind of woman. And she sometimes knew she might have been. One of those really self-sufficient ones with a career of her own. Not little watercress sandwiches. Something she could have worked at, as hard as she had worked at any number of things that never seemed to count somehow in most modern accountings. But she could have lived in this new generation and understood what they kept trying to make her understand – in their books, their articles, the programs she watched. But then, after you understood it all, and God knows, she thought she understood it – the sudden crushing desire to take the oar and be that woman she hadn't been – then what did she understand?

Bert let his arms hang down, reached to hold the edge of the boat, climbed awkwardly into the back seat. Still he couldn't speak, heaved sporadically as he breathed. Then sat dragging his hand in the water. Not taking the oars yet. Not taking the oars at all. Nor starting the motor. Just dragging his hand, watching the tiny bubbles form and break, form and break. Clear, tiny bubbles. He wondered if he had ever noticed them before, what he had noticed before. And he shuddered.

The Train Ride

THE FAT MAN WALKS down the aisle of the train, alert to the empty seats. There are enough of them; he isn't worried. His name is Joe. At least that's what the other drivers call him at the taxi stand where he works.

Halfway through the car, he finds a seat beside an older woman with greying hair who is reading a newspaper. He glances at her and observes what he takes to be a kind face, although she doesn't look at him. He likes to talk and the young girls with headsets and cell phones won't so much as notice him. When he gets on the train at Aldershot where he leaves his car every month or so, there is usually someone who will chat on the trip to Windsor. By Aldershot, the train is usually almost full. Today there are enough seats that he takes his time as he moves forward.

"This seat taken?" he asks.

The woman shakes her head no, keeps on reading. So Joe shoves his black duffel bag in the bin above the seats and closes the overhead door. She doesn't look up as he heaves himself into the aisle seat next to her.

"Today's paper?" he asks.

"Yes," she nods.

He can see that it's *The Globe and Mail*, a Toronto paper.

"Did you get on the train in Toronto?"

She nods.

"You from there?"

"Yes."

She goes on reading and he settles back into the seat. Wants to say, "Name's Joe," but it doesn't feel right. Did he make a mistake? She isn't the least bit interested in chatting. If she were, by now she would have smiled at him, offered him part of her paper. She reminds him a little of his Mama, although she's much older than his Mama was when she died. And not so round. It's the gentleness in her face, the slope of her shoulders. Although all he has to remember Mama by are some black and white photographs and the fleeting impressions of a young child.

When the woman finishes with the newspaper half an hour or so later, she folds it carefully and puts it into her bag. So that's it, Joe thinks. He would like to know who won last night's soccer game.

"Excuse me," she says.

"You want to get up?"

"Umhm."

She walks down the car toward the washrooms, where she stands and peers out the window and then stretches her arms above her head. Looks pretty good for her age, he thinks. Well over sixty. He just hit that milestone a month ago. *Sixty. Hard to believe.* He feels rusty, but not old yet. *That's the way it goes.* Still, he keeps active looking after the garden where he lives in a small apartment in a house, lower rent for taking care of the grass and shovelling snow. His aging landlord lives upstairs with his wife. Below him is a buddy whom he told about the apartment the last time it was empty. He's not sure it was such a good idea. Fred sleeps late because he's afraid if he gets up he'll be bored. Joe can't fathom this. There are so many books to read, so much music to listen to, birds singing everywhere, places to travel. He might be lonely sometimes, but he's rarely bored.

When the woman returns, she asks if he'd like to sit near the window.

"Wherever you like," he says. As if they were travelling together and he wants to please her. He almost never sits in the seat with the best view, knows the terrain well from his many trips along this route, the undulating farm land, the rich earth in the fields, swaying corn, soy bean crops.

"I'd like to sit in the aisle seat."

He doesn't ask her why she didn't take the aisle seat earlier, when she left Toronto. Instead she sat where she had invited company, not leaving anything on the seat beside her that might suggest otherwise. It was misleading and he feels annoyed with her. He settles in next to the window, conscious of the fat rolling out over his belt in large circles. Like jelly, he heard a child say one day. He wheezes as he tries to make himself more compact so he doesn't overflow onto her side. Her body leans toward the aisle. She takes some typewritten pages from her bag, unfolds them on her lap and starts to mark the first page with a ball-point pen. He studies the marks surreptitiously over her shoulder. Reminds him of high school, a teacher who encouraged him to write, said his essays were good. The red pen strokes corrected his grammar, but also circled phrases the teacher liked. Images. For a while, he loved Miss Cassidy. Now he thinks she was probably the best teacher he ever had, though he never wrote anything other than the essays he had to turn in for assignments. But he read a lot and still reads as much as he can; maybe he got that from her. Miss Cassidy came from the Midwest, outside Chicago somewhere, to his high school in Buffalo. She wore neatly pressed blouses and pendants with animals in the centre, symbols. He must have been about fourteen at the time, liked playing football more than studying. But he read at night in his room under a desk lamp with a long gooselike neck. And he was devastated when he learned the next fall she'd left to marry some bloke in Texas.

Joe tries to read the title on the page the woman is marking, but he can't make it out.

"You an English teacher?" he asks.

Her arm and shoulder jump, as if she's startled. "No," she says.

"Look like one."

"Oh."

"I thought you were, the way you're marking that paper."

"I'm editing an article for a friend."

"I love to read," he said. "And in my job, I get lots of time to read."

The train slows down as another freight passes them. He looks out the window and watches it lumber by, waits for theirs to pick up speed again. Wonders if she'll ever say anything.

"What do you like to read?" she asks, looking at him for the first time. He feels her taking in his features, his bulbous nose, the glasses stuck back on his head, a bit tight so that they don't quite reach his ears, the peaked hat with a Harley Davidson motorcycle on it – does she see his cochlear implant? He hears quite well with it, but even after five years it feels odd sometimes. The deafness started when he was still married, but he didn't do anything about it then. He tried to hide it. Talked a lot. Tried to read lips.

"Mysteries," he says. "Dick Francis, John something or other. Grisham. Le Carré. You name it. Has to have a good story, work toward a crescendo, and then surprise me." His body quivers slightly as he speaks, his voice rising in anticipation of conversation. Anything to keep the momentum of the thoughts that tumble out of him. "I like jazz and blues, too. In 1967 went to this place in New York City and you won't believe who was there. Charlie Parker. Thelonius Monk. Fats Waller. Oh, Lordie. So beautiful. Can you imagine?"

"What do you do? How do you get so much time to read on the job?"

"Taxi driver at the Buffalo Airport. Lots of time waiting for fares. The other guys call me the librarian." Joe, the librarian.

She laughs politely as if to say, "Well, that's a good one!"

"Maybe you're a writer." He'd like that. He could read one of her books while he sat in the line-up at the airport.

"No."

"Where are you going?"

"Chatham."

"I'm going to Detroit, get off in Windsor where my daughter will pick me up. She's a good girl. Married, has one son, expecting another baby. I like my son-in-law, too. He's a good sort. I go to visit them often, always take the train. I was married to her mother, but we're divorced. Still good friends, though. She's Canadian. You speak like a Canadian. I can tell from your accent."

The woman looks at him, a slight frown curling the lines between her eyes. "*Je parle français aussi,*" she says with a slight Quebecois accent.

"Oh," he says. "Where you from? Not Toronto really, huh?"

"Yes and no."

"My wife, she came from Montreal, she speaks French. Lives on the south shore now." That Francie, she was pregnant when they married, Francine is her name. Pretty. He was in Montreal for days at a time, driving a truck then. Lived there for a while before Francie and their little girl, Marie, came to Buffalo. "You know that area? The south shore?"

She shakes her head, she doesn't. Knows Montreal, she says.

"Still, you sound like a Canadian," he smiles. "I always think of donuts. Got a thing for them, you folks."

"Really?" She takes out a large green apple and polishes it with a napkin, takes a big bite out of it. "What kind of food do you like?"

"Well, I like a donut now and then. But I like something made with vegetables and herbs. You know, thyme, oregano, what's the one with the wispy stem, lots of green, arugula. I'll give you a recipe for green vegetables, sauteed in hot oil. So good, makes my mouth water to think of it."

"I like arugula."

"And those chips they eat in Quebec, you know, with the cheese."

"Poutine."

"That's it. Poutine. And the pork pies." He can taste them, sighs, quiet then for a while, savouring the thought of the pork pies Francie used to make. And the french fries. His stomach rumbles. Always hungry. Once he started to eat all that rich food, the rolls around his middle expanded. Chocolate, too. Melting on his tongue.

"The guy with the cart been by?" He'll buy something. "Can I treat you to a drink?"

"No, thanks."

"Well, I'm so thirsty, my mouth is dry. Want some water. A coffee. Anything. Soda."

"He'll come by again. He was here just before you got on the train."

She can talk after all. But she stops just as easily, picks up the pages again with her scribbles on them, puts her head down. He feels the fence go up, good neighbours have fences, something like that. Never liked fences.

"Ever been across the ocean?" he asks.

"Um..."

"I love Italy. I've been to Rome, Florence, Venice, Isle of Capri, Sicily. I like Venice, but it's too expensive. Ever been to Italy?"

"No," she says. "Well, Venice once a long time ago."

"Sicily is beautiful. My folks came from there." He wonders why it took him so long to go and see the island where he and his parents were born, his first trip only a couple of years ago. It was beautiful. He went to Mt. Etna, the stark landscape a reminder of an active volcano that last erupted the year before he was there. Many ruins were preserved because they were buried under ash from previous eruptions or under mud from slides. He loved the people, their smiling faces, their kindness, their sense of humour. His father had worked on the trains so he was away a lot. After his mother died, when his father travelled for work he left Joe, an only child, with his large family of sisters and brothers.

"Are you Italian?"

"You bet. Joe's the name I'm known by. But I'm Mario Vincente Russo." He says the words with a flourish and an Italian accent.

She turns and looks at him more closely. "Oh," she says, as if Italian hadn't dawned on her. He thinks she might tell him her name, but she doesn't. "Where do you drive from the airport?" she asks.

"All over," Joe says. "I had a fare last week to New York City. Woman had to get there by a certain time. Paid me a thousand."

"That's a lot of money."

"It's a long way. She was in a hurry."

She turns away from him again, pulls out a book from her bag. If she buries her nose in that, that'll be the end of chatting. But he can't think of anything else to say. She hands him the newspaper.

"Want this?" she asks.

"Thanks." Joe takes it and pulls out the sports section. "I want to know the soccer scores."

"I guess Brazil's still in."

"Yes."

He likes Toronto where all the teams get cheered. All along College Street, St. Clair. Italian flags. Portuguese flags. Was there one for Ghana? Maybe. You find every colour, language in Toronto. He tells her as if she wouldn't know.

"Great city," he says.

She stands up.

"You getting off here?" he asks.

"Not yet."

"Not going through to Windsor?"

"No."

Joe's disappointed. He'd forgotten she'd mentioned a city that came before Windsor a short while ago. And she's just starting to talk to him. Probably interesting. Knows what he's talking about, the herbs, the jazz, the books, all of it.

"Going to see family?"

She nods. "It's my granddaughter's eighth birthday today. I'm going to the party."

"Me, too," he says. "It's my grandson's fifth birthday on Monday."

She smiles, reaches for her bottle of water. Sips it and screws the lid on again.

"I have a cochlear implant." Joe points behind the ear closest to her, his right ear. His mother didn't listen to him when he was little, always talked over his voice. Maybe she was deaf, too. She died when he was almost eight and he hadn't thought before that a loss of hearing might have been the reason she seemed to ignore him.

"I didn't notice," she says.

"It's new, just five years ago." He works with others who've had the implants since. It's like a miracle to be able to hear again, but he thinks sometimes he talks too much. Maybe she would have said more if he hadn't. No, she was determined not to. He could tell. Like his mother. Sometimes his Mama just wanted him to leave her alone. He wants to tell the woman about his Mama, but he figures he would see little lines of disapproval tighten her face and her eyes would glance away. Women never want to hear about how his Mama died and left him alone in the world. Even Francie had said to *ferme* his *bouche.*

"So how do your clients reach you?" she asks. "Do you advertise at the airport?"

Joe pulls his beeper from his pocket. If someone calls it will reverberate against his leg and when he pulls it out, a number will show. "I don't have a telephone," he says. Fred did, just down the stairs from him. "But I use a buddy's when I get messages on this." A hangover from the days when he couldn't hear, he thinks. But it still serves him well and he doesn't have to pay a monthly telephone bill. To keep in touch with his friends, he uses the Internet and e-mail at a coffee shop. He likes to think that he moves with the times, he says.

The conductor goes through the car, removing white tickets from the bins overhead. He's selective, takes only the ones for the next stop each time. This time it will be Chatham. "In about five minutes," he says.

The woman stands and reaches up to the rack above for her pack.

"Need help?" Joe asks.

"It's okay," she says as the bag comes sliding out and down. She puts it on her seat and stands in the aisle.

"I enjoyed our conversation," he says.

"Thanks," she says. "I did, too."

"Be well," he says. "Be happy. Enjoy your granddaughter's birthday."

A smile lights up her face for the first time in their dialogue and Joe thinks he wasn't wrong after all, she has a kind and open face. She probably just wanted to read her newspaper and book and that article her friend wrote. It was probably hard for her not to talk with him; she has a flicker of interest in her eyes now.

"You enjoy your grandson, too," she says.

Then she walks down the aisle toward the exit behind a line of people. She leans over and scans the faces below the window. Joe can't tell whether she's seen anyone or not; she doesn't wave. After a while, the line moves forward and she is lost from view. He peers out the window and soon sees her walk along the platform. She didn't tell him her name. Not even her first name. He feels a stab of envy when he sees her greeted by a tall man and woman and a young fair-haired girl in a blue and white dress who leaps toward her. The woman bends her knees until she is at the level of the child and the little girl, smiling, puts her arms around her grandmother's neck. Joe looks longingly at them.

When the train starts, he looks back once. By now the woman is handing her bag to the tall man and they are walking toward a green stationwagon. It will be another hour to Windsor. Joe wishes his daughter were really going to meet him there. He doesn't know where Marie is any more. She's stopped calling, stopped answering his letters. And Francie's been dead for a while now. He feels tears in his eyes and squeezes his lids together until they subside. He supposes he'll buy lunch somewhere in Windsor and wander around for a few hours before the evening train pulls out, heading back toward Toronto. He won't go far, just to Aldershot. Before that, maybe he'll have another conversation. Or maybe he won't. Then he'll get off the train, find his car in the parking lot, and drive back to Buffalo.

The man with the cart approaches again, the same one who checked tickets earlier. Aldershot to Windsor.

"Snacks, drinks," he says. "Anything you need?"

Joe doesn't look up, turns instead to look out the window as the train picks up speed. Why does everyone leave him? he wonders. How many people are there like him, alone, without a single soul left in the world who really cares about them? Sooner or later, his daughter will call him, he hopes.

National Personals

JULY 1990

PROF. MALE, 55, 5' 10". Slim, dancer, skier, horseback rider, aspiring writer, with log cabin and private lake in Muskoka, seeks female writer. Reply to Box 3250, The Globe.

Hi!

Why am I answering your ad? I don't even read the "Companions Wanted" section. Or I haven't for ages. How did it happen? Let me see! I guess I started by skimming the job ads in the classified section. It's amazing what an incredible array of possibilities that creates. I could be CEO of a large company or Executive Director of some Health Clinic or a social worker doing intake for a group home. Or a hairdresser. I think there was something in Peterborough. Or I could move to Ottawa and work for the Canada Council. Imagine all the things that I could apply for. It provides wonderful fantasy for fifteen minutes on Saturday morning. And then suddenly I saw the "Companions Wanted" section and there weren't many ads there so I scanned them, too, and yours jumped out at me.

Prof. male. I wonder what the "prof." is. It could be just about anything, I guess. 55. Hmm. About right. Just a little older than me chronologically. (I am 37 in my mind, but I think that was really about 15 years ago.) Your height! Not bad. Slim. I like that. And that you are athletic, although what we do is different. For instance, I stole a horse once, but I didn't even get to ride it or I was afraid to. Or something. By the way, I was eleven. And, the last time I skied I broke my arm and that was cross-country. Still, I cycle, skate, canoe, walk – and I would ski again, I love being out in the country. I grew up where you put on your skis when you went out the back door.

What else? The log cabin! I am hopelessly romantic about cabins and have rented a log one on a lake north of Montreal for a week later in July. And visit another on a Gulf Island whenever I have the chance.

Does that give you a slight picture of someone for whom your ad conjured up images? Even though I am skeptical about meeting anyone even remotely compatible through the newspaper. Aren't you? I mean, what's the matter with me that I have to answer an ad? Or with you that you have to place one? Fishing and networking sometimes work, I guess. Why not give it a whirl? What the heck! Who knows?

Oh yes, I almost forgot, I've had short stories published, but am neither established nor prolific. That I write is simply an important part of who I am.

So, may I have this dance? That is, if you're not already swamped with female writers ready to ride, ski, dance into the sunset of a private lake in Muskoka.

Best wishes, Carolyn (Tel. 332-3313)

October 1990

> *EXECUTIVE interested in nature, travel, gardening, theatre, art and planet earth wishes to meet a kind, intelligent, very attractive lady to help plan and build a home and garden at a place still to be determined. I am a very useful N/S 58-year-old, tall, trim, easy going, and financially secure who has learned to be caring. If you would like a quiet lifestyle interspersed with interesting trips, please send a long letter about yourself with photo and phone no. to Box 3742, The Globe and Mail, 444 Front Street West, Toronto, Ontario M5V 2S9.*

Hi!

Every so often I read the "Companions Wanted" section if I happen across it on a Saturday. The last time was in July. It is almost November. Where does time go? That captures life these days as well as any other metaphor.

So … Your ad! Why that one and not some other? Why now and not last month or next month? Serendipity, I guess. Anyway, it was the ad that jumped out at me that said, *Answer this one.* None of them might have, of course. That's another possibility. So why did it? A quiet life style! The time I spend walking in the country or sitting beside a lake or river is precious. And there isn't enough of it. So I stop to watch leaves fall in the city as I walk or ride my bicycle down quiet streets and lanes. Or over on the island.

But I meander. I appreciate that you acknowledged that you have learned to be caring. Because what interests me is a man who is in touch with who he is and so can be genuinely caring.

Now let me tell you a bit about me. I'm a non smoker, 52 years old, trim, slim, fit, interested in art (I enjoy visiting galleries when I travel), theatre, music, canoeing, cycling. What else? I grew up in a mining town up north, next to the bush. Nature and the outdoors were a way of life. I put on my skis at the back door in winter and picked blueberries a few minutes from home in the summer. The town was predominantly French and I still manage reasonably well in French after an hour or two of exposure. I am not an avid gardener, but I have begun in recent years to enjoy my garden more and suspect I would enjoy sharing that kind of work/leisure activity.

I write fiction and have had short stories published. I also work as a counsellor on a crisis line. My two children are in their twenties and have their own lives, although we are good friends.

I have lived in Toronto for thirty years and am happy and comfortable here, but I have always known that I could leave. While I have no burning desire to do so at the moment, I am open to possibility. For it seems to me that what holds people together are the dreams they have in common and planning and creating a home and garden and a quiet lifestyle interspersed with interesting trips is a dream I would happily share. I have realized dreams also which are individual ones, to write stories, to play with colour, and to travel alone in places where I didn't know the language. Now I am ready to share a lifestyle that appreciates what each person brings to it and that offers opportunities for growth not possible alone.

I'm sorry I don't have a photograph to send, but I'm prepared to meet you without seeing one of you. I AM attractive so I hope you will risk meeting me on my say so.

I'm also interested in planet earth, in what we can do to save it – on a very small scale as well as on the larger political one.

Best wishes,

Carolyn (332-3313)

January 1991

The short response to your ad is:

Female, 52. Loves theatre, art, music, hiking, walking, cycling, canoeing, yoga. Would probably still love dancing, but haven't danced for a while. Works as a crisis counsellor, but writes fiction and dabbles with watercolours as well. Grew up in northern town and loves the outdoors. Likes cross-country skiing, probably needs refresher and lots of patience. Has never wind-surfed, but who knows? Doesn't drink or smoke. Reply Carolyn, 332-3313.

July 1991

Hi!

As a woman who writes fiction and plays with watercolours, I would be delighted to meet a happy, single man who appreciates what it means to be in touch with one's creativity.

I am 53, also slim, fit and active, like my life (somewhat eclectic, possibly eccentric), which consists of friends, grown kids, work in the social services (job share), cycling, yoga, walking, music, cinema, etc. All of this surrounds and nourishes the creative core where I struggle with my art with a mixture of joy, pain, delight, and wonder.

If these words hit respondent chords, please call Carolyn, 332-3313.

September 1991

Hi!

I'm interested in what you think the ingredients for a "*truly great relationship*" are. It's what I also want now, when, at 53, I feel more together in body, mind, and spirit than I previously knew was possible. What a wonderful place to be, happy with life and able to share humour, warmth, care.

What else? Yes, I'm also healthy, intelligent, attractive, slim, fit, with eclectic interests (art, music, cycling, walking, yoga, travel, etc.) and the energy (if not always the time) to pursue them.

For the record, I don't smoke, am 5'6", and weigh 122 pounds.

If these words hit respondent chords, please call.

Carolyn (332-3313)

November 1991

Hello.

It's likely rash for me to respond to your ad as I'm not sure I'm ready to uproot myself from an active, interesting life and enter into my "golden years" yet. At 53, I feel young at heart, am active, fit, and frequently forget I am older than 42 or 47 or even, sometimes, 37. Having said that, we share common interests – music, art, nature, the outdoors. Perhaps others. A desire for companionship, harmony. So I'm writing anyway. It also appears that you live in the vicinity of my daughter and son-in-law who live near Lake Huron where I have gradually begun to feel some sense of connection over the five years they have been there.

So, I am 5'6", slim, attractive, intelligent, creative, with eclectic interests and a sense of fun and humour. I live a healthy lifestyle – non-smoker, non-drinker, walk a lot, do yoga, cycle. I have had a few short stories published and am working on a novel, dabble in water colours and job share in a social service agency. I speak only one and a half languages, but listen in fascination to others and often understand a few words. I'm interested that you know four plus. Does that mean you come from a European country such as Switzerland or the Netherlands? Or does it imply a career that involved living in different parts of the world? Or? The half language I know comes from an upbringing in northern Quebec where I was surrounded by the sounds of French. I have lost a lot of what I once knew (fluent in my teens), although from time to time I find myself in environments where it gradually re-emerges.

I could go on, but that gives you some idea. If you are interested in talking and perhaps arranging to meet somewhere, you may call me at 332-3313.

Carolyn

January 1992

Hi.

The most pressing question is – which teeth have you retained? Since what you invite is correspondence, I guess it doesn't really matter if the ones at the front are missing! I do have compatible characteristics, including most teeth (I have some crowns and a bridge in lieu of the others), two offspring (late twenties), hair, and if not always witty, have an irreverent sense of humour. And eclectic interests that more or less include the ones you mentioned. Although on Saturday I usually go to the market and miss the Met, an omission which does not reflect a lack of interest in music so much as a desire to eat for the rest of the week.

Ah so! It is likely foolhardy to write to you just when I have concluded ads are not the way to meet a man, that whoever I am intended to meet will appear as I go about enjoying my rather hectic life, likely when I least expect it. But I am an inveterate reader of the *Globe*'s "National Personals" and your ad intrigues me. Also writing letters sounds like an interesting way to get to know someone even if the geography ultimately proves impossible for anything other than correspondence.

So, at 53, I feel young at heart, and am active and fit. I am 5'6", slim, attractive, intelligent, creative. I live a healthy, casual lifestyle – am a non-smoker, walk a lot, do yoga, cycle. I enjoy the outdoors and have found ways to nurture that in spite of living in a major metropolitan area. I have had short fiction published and am working on a novel, play with watercolours and job share in a social service agency.

I grew up in northern Quebec and have lived in Toronto for most of my adult life. I have studied at different times at McGill, U of T and Simon Fraser. What else? I enjoy many authors, but can usually only wax eloquent about the ones who have made the most recent impression. Last fall, I read 3 novels by William Maxwell that I particularly enjoyed. You may have seen the article in the *Globe* that described him as a writer Alice Munro claimed as an influence, also as a long time editor of the *New Yorker*. I like Alice Munro's work. Nino Ricci's *Lives of the Saints*, Adele Wiseman's *Old Woman at Play*, Joy Kogawa's *Obasan*, Thomas Berger's *Fragile Freedoms*. Margaret Laurence's work has always moved me. W.O. Mitchell's *Who Has Seen the Wind*? Anything by Timothy Findley. I liked Ernest Buckler's well-known novel, to name one Maritime writer. I forget the title though. I could go on. If you respond, I likely will!

I visited Halifax once and found its beauty crept up on me quietly. I have always been attracted to the west coast with the high drama of the mountains scratching the sky and the Pacific pounding against the rocks. The gentler beauty of the east and the rootedness of the people, the sense of history and community, were very appealing. Is that still so or have the miseries of the recession, the effect of the FTA, the fears of separation, etc. changed the atmosphere in a significant way?

That's probably enough to give you some flavour of who I am. What about you? Which authors do you enjoy? How is your interest in ecology expressed in your life? I haven't listened to CBC's *Ideas* for a while, but what they talk about interests me. Tell me about your one offspring. I have a daughter and a son. What kind of work do you do? What artists do you like? Movies? Do you like to travel? Where? When I travel, I usually visit art galleries, spend some time near water, and watch people, among other things. I could go on, but if I don't stop now, I'll burn my dinner.

I hope to hear from you.

Best wishes,

Carolyn (Box 324, Stn. X, Toronto)

September 1992

TORONTO academic, divorced, middle-aged, slim, fit, not bad-looking surrounded by earnest male scientists, wonders where the brainy women are hiding. Reveal yourselves! Box 3032, The Globe and Mail, 444 Front St. West, Toronto, Ont. M5V 2S9.

Hi!

I haven't been hiding, but since you're surrounded by men and I'm surrounded by women, it isn't surprising we haven't met.

I'm also divorced, middle-aged, slim, fit and not bad-looking. I write fiction and work as a counsellor in a service for women. I enjoy theatre, music, cycling, yoga, walking, travel, raking leaves! I'm casual, creative, intelligent, and independent.

I seek the warmth and growth of sharing with a man who is young at heart, comfortable with himself, who has diverse interests and a sense of humour.

The closest I come to academe these days is a son who is studying math in Germany at the graduate level. I also was close enough to touch (I didn't) Stephen Hawking at the Banff Centre for the Arts this spring.

I would be pleased to hear from you, Carolyn (332-3313).

GETTING TO KNOW YOU PARTY. Join up to 300 other Singles for our "Getting-to-know-you-party" on November 14, 1992. Maybe Ms. or Mr. Right will be standing right beside you. Everyone coming to the event will have his or her own CODE name.

CODE NAME: VOYAGE
OCCUPATION: Writer/Counsellor
LIKES: Fresh air, yoga, cycling, the arts, alfalfa sprouts, learning, travel
DISLIKES: Smoking, red meat, arrogance
FAVOURITE MOVIE: *Casablanca*
PREFER TO BE: On vacation
WHY: Ready to relax
MR. RIGHT: Comfortable with self, flexible, diverse interests, sense of humour, fit
SEEKING: Middle-aged man, young at heart, tired of singles

events & newspaper ads, ready for a different voyage.

Carolyn met a Roman Catholic priest at a funeral in Kingston who offered to drive her back to Toronto. She thanked him and said she would be delighted as long as he didn't try to convert her. After an hour in the car, he called her a seeker and told her he also practised yoga. He gave her the name of his therapist before he let her off at the subway. She didn't know how to tell a Roman Catholic priest that she found him interesting and would really like to see him again.

He called to return the umbrella she left in his car, but he left it on her front porch and she didn't hear from him again after she called to thank him. But the phone rang twice in the following week, ads she had answered and forgotten. One man taught survival skills to the military and was off to go hot air ballooning in New Mexico. He would like to meet her when he returned. "This is the 'Snowbird' from the *Globe*," the other said. They met for coffee and talked for two hours. He looked like a Viking, had a boat in Curacao, and had spent three years in a concentration camp in Indonesia during the Second World War. He had 62 replies to his ad.

"Have you ever met anyone like this before?" he asked. "Through an ad?"

"Yes," she said.

"It could be a full-time job," he said. "This business of meeting people."

When she returned from the washroom before they left the restaurant, she found him jotting notes in a little black book.

"Did I get an A or a B?" she asked.

"I was just noting that you're writing a book and backpacked in Europe."

"So you won't get everyone confused," she laughed.

"Yes," he said. "You know, when I thought of placing an ad and making arrangements to meet strangers, I thought it would be such a strain. I was looking forward to finding a companion. But I'm meeting such interesting people – I like this part of it."

"Hmhm," she said.

EPILOGUE

December 1992
Carolyn composed two ads:

CREATIVE female, 54, N/S, active, attractive. Fed up with singles' scene and reading the "National Personals." Invites replies from warm, literate, gentle, caring, middle-aged man with a sense of humour and some of the following, or compatible, interests – nature, walking, cinema, music, art, theatre, travel, social justice, savoury food, good conversation, even marriage. Reply: C., Box 324, Stn. X, Toronto

INVETERATE liar (writes fiction), this gal learned to steal horses young (eleven), now lives healthy life style sans cigarettes and alcohol, eats alfalfa sprouts and avoids red meat. Seeks literate fellow adventurer, 47 to 58 1/2, who likes theatre, music and art, and can laugh at life's follies and travel by bicycle or canoe as well as in first class when the spirit moves him, for a lifelong saga yet to be written. Cast your fate to the wind! Carolyn. Box 324, The Globe and Mail. No replies to racist, sexist bores.

Carolyn placed both ads and had more replies than she knew what to do with. So she set up a filing system. Would she file them by name or by interests? Aspirations and dreams? It was a quandary. There were a couple of obscene letters she ripped up and threw in the wicker wastebasket beside her desk. It was only when she found that one man had answered both ads, different letters that suited each one, quite imaginative, too, that she decided that was enough reason to contact someone. When they met for dinner, she discovered it was the Viking. He told her that despite his system, he had lost her number.

"I did want to call you again," he said.

And, tired of trying to keep track of all the women he'd met, he decided to answer a couple of new ads instead. Funny, both were hers.

"Which of the two ads did you prefer?" she asked.

"I liked both of them," he said.

"Hmmm...."

February, 1993

"I'd like to take a trip," Carolyn wrote to her friends. "I've finally decided to give up on the personals! If you hear of anyone with an apartment to spare or rent for three or four weeks in Paris, London, NYC, Rome, Florence, Barcelona ... Montreal perhaps? You could say that I'm exploring. Or you could say that I'm fishing. You get the picture! New Mexico, for that matter. Please let me know. Or for a couple of weeks in St. John's (probably September on that one). I'm also looking for someone to share expenses. Male or female. Spread the word. I'm open to anything. Might lead to a good story.

Much love..."

Neighbours

PASSERS-BY SOMETIMES SPOKE to Dick and Tony when they worked in their garden. They admired the changes the two men had made to the house on Crandale Avenue – the gas light, the ivy climbing up the foot of it – but the two men generally kept to themselves. Although gradually they, as well as their cars, one of them a grey Toyota Camry, parked at the curb under the birch in the front yard, became fixtures.

To the east of them was a newly married couple and I lived on the other side, a divorcee with grown children. Dick and Tony had known the children since they were eight or ten or twelve or so. My then husband moved out within months of Dick and Tony's arrival. They had only met him briefly and nodded to each other from time to time before that. It was when Dick was in hospital after an operation on his bowel, all knotted somehow inside like a rope, that he told me about what he referred to as his *lifestyle*. He didn't tell me then about the blood test as I sat like Florence Nightingale beside his bed, holding his hand. I realized later that he couldn't think about it himself yet.

A year or so later, when he could no longer work for the bank, Dick told the people he worked with that he had leukemia. Apparently one or two of them said they would visit. He was noncommittal, but when one woman called he asked Tony to go out. Maybe his colleagues knew about Tony, but he didn't think so. He had always been discreet; he said he had to be in his kind of business. As for what he had, the terror that invaded his body, only their closest friends knew for sure. Except me, the one neighbour they told that it wasn't leukemia.

"The front door's open," they said. "Come over whenever you want."

So I walked right in. "Hello," I hollered.

Dick's voice from overhead was weak and sleepy.

"It's all right," Tony said from the kitchen, his head peering around the corner like a small boy's. "Go on up. He likes to see you."

Although it wasn't always true. There was the time after they put the black wrought iron fence up in the front when we glared at each other. Then later when they built the addition, it felt like a fortress they'd constructed with lines drawn in the sand between us. Iraq and Iran. At war again. But by then it was all right and had been for a long time.

"I'm coming up," I called, nodding at Tony.

The stairs were covered with brown carpet, soft as clouds of satin, and the wall beside them was exposed brick. As I reached the landing, I saw the red panels Dick brought back from a palace in Vietnam, hanging proudly as if still in their original, grand setting. Dick always called it *the* palace, but with my vague memory for historical detail and not being American (he came to Toronto after that war), the significance was lost on me. I told him his stories about Vietnam made me think of bombs falling. *Dead in Haiphong. Dead in Saigon.*

Dick lay curled up like a baby under a navy blanket on his wooden, four-poster bed, the mirror overhead reflecting how thin he'd grown. The leaves on the birch outside, which I could see through the open wooden shutters of the window, had begun to turn yellow. The window was surrounded with ivy. A breeze blew and a few golden leaves floated by in an arc before plummeting downward.

I gave Dick the food I had brought before sitting on the chair at the end of his bed, resting my arms on the wooden armrests. The last time I visited he told me his mother had cooked squash when he was a child, pork sausage in the middle flavouring it right through to the rind. Before his mother knew he was gay, before she said any son of hers who was *that way* might just as well be dead. He left home right after high school – disowned, disinherited – to join the military. His father said, "Just you wait, the army will shape you up when they get you." The army *was* hard, but he stayed in Vietnam for two and a half years, longer than he had to. He always said this with pride, although he knew I had been anti-Vietnam and my latest boyfriend arrived in Canada years earlier to avoid the draft. What he liked was that, even so, I listened as he recounted his history.

"I knew the general," he said more than once. "And I had access to secret information and deciphered high-level messages. Once I was used as a decoy to keep the general from being shot."

Although he would have been aware that this story was like *the* palace and I would have forgotten which general.

Dick leaned over now and picked up a spoon from a bowl on the floor. "You remembered." He started to eat the yellow squash. When he put the spoon down, he smiled. "I feel better now that I have my funeral planned," he said.

I had listened to each stage of the arrangements over the past weeks when Tony was the only other person who would listen. I thought of the wasp hidden under the leather jacket I carried over my arm as I walked up a road the previous year in Grindelwald. Suddenly when I shifted, the wasp stung me. It was after I returned from Switzerland, in June, that Dick told me on the lawn in front of the house that he was HIV positive. Even though I had visited him in the hospital after the operation a year and a half earlier and known he was frail, my first impulse was that he was lying. I stared at him. *That's not what you told me.* As far as I knew, he was much better since that operation.

"You promised you'd trim the flower bed next to the fence," I'd said. "When I get older." I knew my words were preposterous.

"You'll be able to come and visit me in the cemetery," he said now. He and Tony had bought a big plot and Tony would plant a small garden around his grave where I could go and picnic. I breathed in deeply and then sighed. I remembered sitting by his bed in the hospital, holding his hand, remembered him apologizing for never having talked openly before.

"I still don't know what to think when the Bible says it's evil," he said that day.

He had never been out, although he was part of the fraternity.

Cape Cod, Key West – places he and Tony visited. Still, it was elliptic, his disclosure.

"It's all right, Dick," I said. "I've always known, but I never said anything because you didn't."

Then he talked of doing things that stretched off into the future. He and Tony were in their mid-forties, almost ten years younger than I was. They always seemed so young to me, fit and energetic. Well put together also – white polo neck sweaters, dark jackets, sleek, freshly-pressed trousers. Even when he was gardening, Dick looked smart, neat in his shorts and expensive t-shirt.

A few days later, Tony told me the same thing about Dick's prognosis. I nodded then. So it was true after all. If I heard it often enough, maybe I would believe it. "How about you?"

"I'm HIV positive, too." He went into a long explanation about T-cells and numbers. The number for him was somewhere in the mid-four hundreds. Dick's was seven. "Oh shit!" I said. And we stood there on the lawn with our arms around each other.

One evening, Dick knocked on my door. He sat at the table overlooking the garden.

"I've just been to see the doctor," he said. "I'm dying." As if he had forgotten I knew already. He cried and I hugged him. When he stopped sobbing, we talked for almost two hours. That night I scarcely slept and when I did, I had nightmares. About wars. About bodies.

The next day, Dick was working in his garden, carefully trimming the edge of the grass and the hedge, cleaning the bronze on the gaslight. For a moment, I thought maybe the nightmare was when he came over and sat at the table, my dream the reality.

"Do you miss your mother?" he asked now from the bed.

I reached over and took the plate from him, empty except for the rind. "Yes, of course," I said.

My mother was determined to keep on living and pulled her bell for someone to come even an hour before the final moment. When I last saw her, her mouth had fallen open as if a hinge had broken. Her eyes stared at the ceiling. She looked surprised.

"She was a great lady," Dick said wistfully.

I remembered the Christmas when Tony went to visit his family and my mother and Dick sat polishing my tarnished silver, both my children still living at home then. I remembered that Tony's parents hadn't known he was gay either, still didn't know.

"Things don't taste the same any more," Dick said. "And I can't see out of this eye," pointing to his right eye. "I have decisions to make about what drugs to take and whatever I decide, I'll still die."

"I'll miss you, too," I said.

When I finally got up to leave, Dick's eyes were vibrant and he was smiling again. "I sometimes forget that year when we didn't speak to each other," he said. After I objected to the plans for the addition to their house. Designs drawn by an architect. A hearing at City Hall about variances from the zoning bylaw. A lawyer represented Dick and Tony and neighbours voiced their objections. I voiced mine and when the application was finally turned down, Tony said angrily that they would sell. Within twenty-four hours, there was a FOR SALE sign on the lawn.

A few weeks later, the sign came down and an extension was built that summer. Within the zoning bylaw. No deck. No windows overlooking my back yard. Eventually an uneasy truce when Dick gradually acknowledged that although I could be prickly, he might be also.

"I almost bought pink flamingos to put on your lawn in the middle of the night," I said. "To surround the FOR SALE sign."

"What do you think?" he asked now. "I keep thinking I'd like to hire a string quartet to come and play for me."

"I'm not sure what you mean."

"Downstairs. In the living room."

It was the first time in a while he had thought about much besides getting his will written and choosing a tombstone. "But I'm worried about what people might think."

He was always confident that whatever he did was in good taste, so I was surprised.

"It sounds wonderful. Quite wonderful."

"I always enjoy our little chats," he said.

Shortly after that, he took a turn for the worse and two friends, both named Michael, left their downtown apartment to help take care of Dick. The string quartet never materialized. I went over just as often, but Dick was worse and couldn't talk as much, and one of the Michaels was almost always right there in the room. So it could have been his failing health or it could have been the Michaels' lingering presence, but whatever it was, Dick stopped telling me stories. Although he told me about the crest he was going to give to one of the sons of his Vietnam buddy and about conversations with *The Reverend* to make sure all the details were in place for his funeral. One day he said that the night before he had crawled out of bed and had gone out into the street. He walked to the architect's house a few doors away and fell down on the grass. When dawn came and birds started to chirp, he made the call he used to invite cardinals to the birdbath in his garden. He said the red bird appeared on the hedge. I wondered if it really happened, but I didn't say so.

Not long after that, he only came to for a minute or so at a time. He moaned in pain in his sleep, he wore diapers, he got thinner and thinner.

"It's why they call it the wasting disease," Tony said.

Dick was on fluids only by now, the morphine had been stopped. It wouldn't be very long. The next day, from my front window I could see a stream of cars and people coming and going, visiting Dick before it was too late. I watched "the girls" arrive, as Tony and Dick called them, the ones who went to office parties with one or the other of them. Lily was the one who went home with Tony for family visits.

The following day, Sunday, when I looked out and saw the hearse, I grabbed my coat and rushed over, my heart pounding. One of the Michaels put his arm around my shoulders, not the one who was usually in the room, the other one.

"He got to see the leaves turn red and golden one last time," I said. "He said he wanted that."

"Yes," Michael said.

We stood in the living room with the friends I'd met at all the celebrations in the last year, all the occasions everyone knew might be the last, like his birthday. That evening, Tony had driven Dick and me in the Camry with snow blowing across the highway to a house somewhere beyond Oakville. It was a modern house with an indoor swimming pool. The downstairs floors were covered with large Oriental carpets. After toasts with glasses of wine, a big cake on the dining room table was unveiled and Dick blew out the candles, momentarily looking as if his wish was about to be granted. Then a shadow crossed his face. Now the friends who were at that party watched two men carry Dick downstairs in a dark bag, all zipped up. It was almost flat.

Tony was in the basement recreation room with Lily. He was upstairs before that with the minister, the Michaels, and two of the girls for the final moments, but he couldn't bear to watch Dick being carried out in the bag.

"It's all right," the lawyer said to me in his loud, booming voice. "Dick would want us to smile."

Michael held me tighter. "It's been terrible, listening to these people who can't show how sad they feel," he whispered.

Tears ran down my cheeks. I wiped them away when Tony came into the room and went over and hugged him. We held onto each other for a long time. When everyone left, I stayed to answer the telephone. It kept on ringing. One of the girls was marching in the AIDS march. For Dick. She was on her way over.

On the day of Dick's funeral, in a big church on Bloor Street, the strings appeared, an entire twelve-piece ensemble.

"Everything was just the way Dick would have wanted it," Tony said at the graveside. "The music in the church, the bagpipes here, the flowers." He looked thin and haggard.

All the friends, till now sworn to secrecy, wore red ribbons. They hovered around Tony. He looked the way Dick did just after I came back from Switzerland. How long did he have? Six months? A year? A year and a half?

In the days that followed, Tony gradually let us all know he wasn't planning on dying yet, that what he wanted was to live alone for a while. He talked a lot about Dick and he cried sometimes. Still, he was going to get rid of all the silver. Dick might have liked it, but he was damned if he was going to waste whatever time was left polishing it. And Dick did all the planning for both their funerals, so now Tony could take a trip. England, Greece, Arizona. Places like that. Most important of all he told me was that he was going to tell his parents about being gay.

"Now that Dick's dead and I'm dying, I'm not going to wait any longer," he said.

His brother and sister attempted to dissuade him.

"It would kill them."

Finally his sister went to Guelph with him for the day. He told me that she walked in the garden while he talked to his parents. His mother took a piece of tissue from her lap and blew her nose. She seemed to be rearranging her features as the lines crumpled and she struggled to sort them out again. She started reminiscing. About the way he was as a little boy.

Tony wanted to scream, he told me.

"Look at me, Mom," he said quietly. "I'm a man. I'm forty-five years old. Dick and I lived together for almost twenty years. He was the most important person in my life. I'm not your little boy any more. And when I was, you didn't know me. I knew from the time I was five years old that I was different."

"Let's talk about something else."

"No."

"How did you meet Dick?"

"On the subway."

"I don't want to hear any more."

"I refuse to lie," he told her. "I loved Dick. I want you to know that."

His father sat quietly. Tears rolled down his mother's face. "You always came for holidays," she said. "You brought Lily."

"Yes," he said. "But even you could see that was all a lie. Now I have AIDS. I want you to know me before I die."

"It's all because of Dick," she said. "I never liked Dick. If it weren't for him, this wouldn't be happening."

"It wasn't Dick's fault."

His mother cried loudly. "It *was* all his fault," she said between sobs. "It's *all* his fault. You wouldn't be sick. You would be married if he hadn't come along. You'd have children. I remember all your girl friends."

His father wouldn't look at him. That's what he always did, gazed off in some other direction when his mother was talking. He never knew if his father agreed with her or was too timid to contradict her. Tony got up and walked out to the garden. "Take me home," he said to his sister.

"What's the matter?"

"Take me home."

In his own yard where I found him later, he was holding his book about "*coming out*" –

"What good did all the preparation do?" he said, tossing it into the wicker basket beside his chair. "I felt as if I was talking to a cement wall. Maybe some time I'll write a letter."

Dear Mom and Dad, I've had to hide my life from you for years. I don't want to do that any more...

But Tony didn't write the letter. He grew thinner and weaker and was increasingly in pain. He could scarcely walk some days. Although he managed to arrange for new windows at the back of the house and planned what he would plant in the garden. Some of the colourful plants Dick never liked. He imagined a fine summer evening when his parents would drive in from Guelph and they would talk. This time their faces would be understanding, like they were when he was a small child.

Instead, Tony caught pneumonia and had a fever.

"We won't put him in hospital," Lily said.

One of the Michaels moved back into the house.

When the fever went down, Tony told me he had weak lungs. "Weaker than Dick's because I was a smoker until a year ago."

"I've been talking to Dick," he said. "Telling him there are still things I want to do here before I join him. I tell him to go find a house and get it ready, but not to rush about it."

His parents came in their big black Oldsmobile. His brother's little blue sports car was there the day after. His sister came on the subway most of the time. Sometimes she sat on the end of his bed and talked and sang quietly to him. His brother wore a red ribbon, but his parents talked about leukemia and taking him home to look after him.

"I'm staying right here," Tony said.

He wanted to die in his own bed, like Dick did. Although if he had to, he would go into hospital. The fever was down now though, so the doctor had stopped saying he should. He was glad because he still had hibiscus to plant in the garden. Bright red. He had ordered new furniture for the living room, too. Lily had taken him to an upscale shop down on King Street. He'd known Lily for a long time. Even before he met Dick, Tony knew her.

"I want the garden filled with hibiscus this summer," he told me. "And a fireplace in the extension because it's cold in there and that's where I want to sit on cool evenings in the fall and winter." He didn't say if I didn't like it, it was too bad. We both knew there was nothing in any bylaw that said he couldn't do it.

With Lily's help, Tony managed to find a contractor to put in the fireplace. They had to cut a hole in the wall and nail wood around the part that extruded over the walk, the part that I could see from my sunroom window.

"How does it look?" he asked.

He was so frail now. Weak. Thin. Cheeks sunken. On the street when I saw prematurely old men shuffling along, I thought AIDS.

"It looks better on the inside," I said. "It looks beautiful on the inside." I didn't say Dick would have been appalled by what I could see from my window, that it was ugly. Or that after the CN Tower it was likely the largest free-standing phallic symbol in Toronto.

"I can lie on the couch and watch television with the gas fire burning," Tony said.

One morning not long after, Michael's head popped up at the top of the fence, almost like Humpty Dumpty, startling me.

"Tony died last night," he said.

I felt the same disbelief I felt when I first heard that Dick was HIV positive.

And Tony never did see the ugly pipe on the outside. Or have a chance to enjoy the hibiscus.

"*O Captain! My Captain*" was printed on the card for his requiem Eucharist, as well as a letter Tony had written to his family. *Once upon a time there was a little boy who had a special secret that he kept very close to his heart. As the little boy became a young man, he heard a different kind of music* ... The letter told about his soul mate and ended ... *Don't let the sun go down on me. Love, Tony.*

The same chamber orchestra that was at Dick's funeral played the music Tony had loved. Vivaldi. Mozart. Grieg.

Over the summer, the house was empty. I watered the hibiscus. Once in the middle of the night, the alarm went off and the security company sent the police out. Two gardeners, both women, cut the grass and trimmed the bushes. It was almost as if Dick and Tony still lived there. One day I received a call from Tony's mother, whom I'd met for the first time at the funeral parlour.

"It was an awful funeral. Didn't you think so?" his mother asked. "Tony's brain must have been affected, he must have been influenced. We'd agreed to call it leukemia."

"His brain was clear," I said finally. "Until the very end." *Oh, Tony, please, am I saying the right thing?* Only the weekend before he died, he used my mother's wheelchair and the Michaels pushed him onto the ferry over to the island and along the boardwalk. He asked for a picnic there. I didn't say that Dick might have been in and out of reality in his final days, but not Tony. With him, it was pneumonia.

Then his mother said it was so awful that her relatives and friends heard at the funeral for the first time about AIDS, that she'd received some horrible phone calls.

In early September, before the leaves turned yellow again, Lily, the lawyer and one of the Michaels came and carefully removed paintings, the stereo, dishes. They gave me a vase and a small Oriental rug. I put the rug on the wood floor in front of my sofa.

Soon after there was a FOR SALE sign on the lawn under the birch tree, a sign that would stay this time until the house was sold. I watched the agent come and go with clients and I could visualize people going through the house and finding it eerie. An estate sale and the only photographs were of young men.

On the day the agent put up a SOLD sign, I walked quickly towards the corner. I didn't want to know yet who bought it. Although I knew there was an offer. The lawyer told me it was someone who liked the garden, someone he thought would take care of it.

Further down the block, closer to Yonge Street, I saw a woman raking leaves into a huge mound and putting them into a clear plastic bag.

"How are you?" she greeted me. Her cheeks were ruddy. "I haven't seen you for a long time."

"I've been around," I said.

"I gather your neighbours won't be for much longer," the woman said. "I just saw the SOLD sign. Do you know where they're going?"

The Essay

SUN SHINES THROUGH THE narrow slats of the white venetian blinds. Only yesterday Natalie thought she might be able to sit at the desk under the window with the light streaming in and finally write the essay. Then the telephone rang. Aunt Berthe was dead of a heart attack. Now she has to decide whether to go to the funeral.

She puts on a kettle of water and takes down a tea bag from a clear glass bottle on the shelf over the spice rack. It's only then that she notices the crayons scattered on the blue tile floor and drawings spread across the kitchen table.

"That damn kid," Natalie mutters. Bonnie always leaves her art out.

She looks at the bright coloured balloons on the sheets of paper she intended to use for her essay. She's taking a course on Quebec literature at the university and working toward another degree. She likes Michel Tremblay and Hubert Aquin. Anne Hébert. She reads the books in translation although she once spoke French fluently. She finds another pad of paper in the cupboard under the cutlery drawer. She thought if she left it there, Bonnie might not find it. She still hasn't decided where to put most things. Her books are in boxes under the window of the tiny apartment. She was lucky to find it. For months, she has been living either in shelters or the homes of acquaintances who offered her a temporary place to stay.

"Until you can find your own," they said.

Now that she has this place, no matter that it's small, that even Aunt Berthe, kind Aunt Berthe who came through with first and last for her, might wonder that this was the best she could do, Natalie wants to keep it. This time she hopes desperately that Bonnie won't spoil it for her. Or Beth, Carolyn, or Catherine either. There are others, but these are the ones Natalie knows best. They turn up and do something when Natalie isn't there and she gets blamed for it. Like the drawings on the walls in the last place. Bonnie really got carried away and drew murals with her crayons all over the apartment. Red flowers on the bathroom wall. A clown with a yellow bulb for a nose in the living room. That was the one that got Natalie out on the street and back into a shelter in less than two hours.

Aunt Berthe sent the money as soon as she heard. She couldn't afford all that much herself, but she would do without something rather than see her niece homeless. She wanted to know why Natalie didn't tell her sooner.

Natalie remembers when her aunt asked her that when she was a child. They were sitting on the porch on the green swing chair.

"What's the matter, Nat?" Aunt Berthe asked. "Why didn't you tell me?"

Natalie doesn't remember why she was crying, but she remembers Aunt Berthe was there for her in a way no one else ever was. Her mother was in hospital off and on and her father away up north in the bush. Hunting. She remembers she didn't mind when her parents were gone because she got to stay with her aunt then. She doesn't remember what she told her aunt that day, and soon learned it was better not to.

The clanking sound of a streetcar going by on tracks below on Queen Street permeates the room. Natalie smiles slightly, she feels safe in the city – she can disappear into crowds, walk along streets where she knows no one. Oh, she supposes after a while she'll talk to people in the shops she frequents. She'll even put down roots of a sort. Superficial because she doesn't really want anyone to know her too well, but she's curious always about her environs and Toronto fascinates her with its distinct neighbourhoods and the endless variety of people she encounters.

Finally she sits down at the table and studies the drawings. The kid's quite talented, but still! Her eyes glaze over as she begins to write on the new pad. This one has lines. She thinks that will stop Bonnie, but then it doesn't stop one of the others.

The words that appear on the page are: *You're all so busy, you don't pay any attention to me. But Aunt Berthe loved me. I want to go to the funeral. I'm not afraid. You're all sissies.*

Beth studies what she has written. The handwriting is large and slants to the left, not at all like Natalie's. She doesn't want to be like Natalie, afraid of her own shadow. Beth leaves the paper on the table and goes to the closet where she takes out a tight black miniskirt and a sweater with sequins on it. Aunt Berthe's eyebrows would go up at the sight of such an outfit, but Beth has always known it didn't change how her aunt felt about her. Impatient, annoyed perhaps, but never loving her any the less.

Beth doesn't like the clothes Natalie wears, thinks she's a bore, always studying. When she finds the essay, Beth rips it up. What's the point of all that work? It's not going to get Natalie anywhere. And if it does, where will Beth be? Beth is fairly certain that if Natalie finishes her courses and starts teaching more it will mean the end of any fun. Natalie has never liked the bar scene or the men Beth brings home. Sometimes she comes out just as the man is about to make love to Beth and scares him away. She calls it rape, tells him to get out of there fast before she calls the cops. The men are always baffled by the sudden change from the happy party girl in the bar.

"C'mon, Beth."

"I'm not Beth," Natalie says.

"You're nuts."

"I'm going to scream," Natalie says.

The trouble is that every once in a while, the men get so angry that Natalie gets raped. Then Beth has to hide for a while and watch stupid Natalie slash her arms with a razor, or bang her head against the wall, as if she's the one to blame. Can't seem to get it through her head that she's not. She doesn't even know what Beth knows except from the notes Beth sometimes leaves for her.

Beth goes into the bathroom and puts on her lipstick and mascara, purple eye shadow. She goes down to the corner pub and sits at the bar with a glass of draft. After a while, she walks across the room to the yellow and black dartboard and pulls out three darts with silver tips and black feathers. The bartender watches her.

"It's quiet today," he says.

She hits the circle outside the bull's eye, between the lines. After the other two darts land outside all the lines, she goes over to the pool table. A man comes over and sits on the edge of it. She ignores him as she takes down a cue.

"What about a game, babe?" he says.

She shrugs and he reaches for a cue as she arranges the balls on the green felt table. She's about to lean over and line up a ball to break up the triangle when she feels very tired.

"Where am I?" Natalie asks.

It's at least two hours since she was aware of the time. Sometimes when she loses time, she's afraid she has gone north. Occasionally she is unaware of what she has done for as long as three days, long enough for Beth, or someone else, to travel to New Liskeard on the train and return again. The Northland is not like the trains she remembers from childhood, just a short train now without a diner or caboose. If anyone went, it would be Beth, she thinks. Unless there's someone she doesn't know yet. Most likely Beth though. But surely if she had gone, Aunt Berthe would have mentioned it in a letter.

Natalie looks at her watch and realizes she'll have to rush to make it to class. She teaches at a community college. She and Carolyn and the rest of them have a job now. Sometimes the students ask why the handwriting on their papers differs from one assignment to another; does someone else mark them?

No, just me, Natalie says. But she knows Carolyn does sometimes. Who knows if one day Carolyn will do something stupid and she'll be out of a job altogether? That's why she wants to finish the essay; she wants to have more options about where she can teach. That's what she told Aunt Berthe on one of her long-distance calls when she first enrolled at the university to work toward a degree.

"That's good thinking, *chérie*," her aunt said.

She still doesn't know if she can go to the funeral. The thought of going back there is frightening, seeing all the relatives, although her father is dead and her mother lives somewhere in the southern states, maybe in Arizona. But she might come back for this funeral, after all Berthe was her sister. For reasons Natalie isn't sure of, she doesn't want to see her mother. What she does know is that whenever she does, she is sick for days and can't manage to do anything. The children do a lot of drawing then, Bonnie in particular, pictures Natalie doesn't want to see sometimes, not like the happy ones she's been drawing recently.

Natalie walks toward the part of the city where she shares an office and where she also teaches, thinking about what she will write about Michel Tremblay. Somehow, his stories are her heritage also, she feels. After all she grew up in northern Quebec, just across the border and north from New Liskeard, and Catherine still speaks French fluently. Natalie only knows Catherine is around because she left a note in French to tell her the essay was too academic, a waste of time. Why doesn't Natalie get the cork out of her ass? the note asked.

"*C'est comme ça,*" Catherine says. She isn't the one who rips up the essay though. She doesn't really care one way or the other if Natalie gets her degree. If she does, maybe Catherine will get more *out* time.

Her office at the college is in an old brick house just off Spadina with three storeys and a large bay window. There's a sign on the door that says *No flyers. No junk mail.* Natalie ignores it as she opens the heavy door and steps inside. Upstairs she looks in a slot to see if there are any messages and discovers that the class she was to give has been cancelled.

Inside her small office, she studies the papers on the desk, counts how many are left to mark. Not many. After she goes through two of them, she gets up and goes to the pile of large red, purple, and green pillows on the floor that the woman she shares the office with has left in the corner. She sits down on one and leans back against the others.

"Oh Aunt Berthe," she murmurs. "Will you mind if I don't make it?"

At the thought, images of rocks and lakes flood her mind. The geography is all that remains from her childhood to soothe her. Now that Aunt Berthe is dead. Dead. She can scarcely fathom it. The last time she remembers being in the north, she walked along the shore of Lake Temiskaming with her aunt and watched the geese fly overhead in large V-formations, honking as they passed above the town.

"Where are the crayons?" the woman leaning against the pillows murmurs. Her voice is childlike. She reaches to pick up a pink pillow and cuddles it as if it were a tiny child or a teddy bear. After a while, she reaches in the bag beside her and takes out a small pad and some pencils.

Bonnie leans forward and starts to draw geese flying across the sky. Then she does a cross on the side of a box on the ground with bright coloured flowers on top of it. She draws a figure with legs apart, dress almost over her head.

"Who's that?" she whispers. She pretends it's Aunt Berthe who is asking her.

"Me," she replies. "It's me."

"What happened?"

"They were all dressed in white skirts," Bonnie says. "They had hoods over their heads. One of the voices sounded like Daddy's. He used to put me in the car when people were coming. I could see through the window."

But she knows she can't say any more. This is the point at which Aunt Berthe will shake her head and say, "You shouldn't make things up, you shouldn't tell lies, you could hurt people." But not nearly as much as what really happened hurt Bonnie, if her aunt would just believe her. Aunt Berthe just doesn't believe that anything that can hurt children so terribly can happen. But the people who came to visit her father and her mother did hurt children. Animals, too. They sat around the table and cut animals up. There was blood. They hurt her cat. She wanted to scream, but her Daddy said if she ever said anything, awful things would happen to her. Like what happened to her cousin, Ruthie.

She's careful not to think what happened to Ruthie because Natalie doesn't know and if she found out MORE awful things would happen. She can draw though. She can draw knives. She doesn't have to tell anyone that they made her cut things up – mice, rabbits – and eat the blood. They put it on where she peed. It hurt her. She starts to cry, to rock back and forth.

"They shouldn't have done that," she whispers. She pretends her aunt is saying it. "No one should ever hurt a little girl like that." Maybe her aunt can do something to stop them. But Berthe is dead now. And all of them may go to the funeral. She doesn't want to go, she's afraid she might get killed there. Like Ruthie. If she only draws but doesn't say anything, maybe Beth and Natalie will find out and they will stay away and no one will get hurt any more. Up until now, they have only seen her drawings of clowns and flowers.

Beth tosses her head back and reaches for a cigarette. She's the tough one, the one who has to take care of all the others. She's sick of it. Although she would rather be tough and not feel anything; she can't get hurt then. If you start to feel, you can't survive getting raped. Or stabbed. She can even watch and remain numb, removed from it all. The weaklings, Natalie and the others, always disappear.

She looks at the papers scattered around her. So the brat has been drawing, she thinks. She goes to the back door and opens it. A clothesline stretches over a car below to a telephone pole. It reminds her of buildings up north covered with brown asphalt shingles, windows covered with plastic, clotheslines where her aunt's towels and sheets froze in the winter. Long ago, Aunt Berthe was poor. Her mother and father laughed when they talked about her.

"Stupid, too," she heard her father say.

She hated her father, grease under his nails and in the lines of his knuckles, his clothes filthy when he crawled out from under a car to fill a gas tank for someone. She remembers those greasy knuckles vividly, like slimy fish that made her shudder when they touched her. She is suddenly sick to her stomach. She can still smell his fingers, smoke lingering on his fingertips mixed with the oil and grease. When he couldn't find her, she would hear his gravely voice.

"Where's the brat gone this time?"

The farther away the better. But he enticed her back with bubble gum and chewy taffy. Back. To the funeral. To the north. There was always a reason.

She looks at the drawings again. If Bonnie drew these, she had to have been there also.

"Oh, Bonnie," Beth sneers. "Little kid. Never grew up." She slams her hand into one of the pillows and then starts scratching her face. She avoids using her nails, but even so there are pink marks across her cheeks. At the same time, she starts to tap one of her feet rhythmically. And to swear. There are pictures of a car that her father used to put her in. Then he would lock the door and leave her there, like a caged animal. Sometimes he left her in the car overnight. There is also a picture of a young girl with a gun to her head. It must be Ruthie, the cousin who shot herself or who someone else shot when she was only four.

Later in the afternoon, Natalie wakes up on the couch in her apartment. She doesn't remember how she got there. Nor does she know if what has just happened was a flashback or a nightmare. She saw a room full of people in long white robes and a baby being killed. Someone in one of the white robes told her it was her sister. She doesn't remember if she ever had a sister. She must have made it up. Or it was a nightmare.

Then she sees the drawings scattered all over the floor. She will have to clean them up so she can start to work on her essay again. As she tears them and stuffs them into the wastebasket, she still thinks what she has just dreamed or remembered could not be real, but what she does know is that something really terrible happened.

"The kids always knew," Bonnie murmurs.

"What?" Natalie says.

Now she'll be depressed all day, she thinks, or have another migraine. That is what happens when Natalie dreams, although usually she doesn't remember the dream itself. She doesn't know if she'll be able to keep from hurting herself. She has a razor. She uses it to cut herself, to get rid of the pain. At the thought of going up north for the funeral, she shivers. Natalie doesn't want to remember anything about what happened when she lived there.

"Why are you crying, *petite*?" Aunt Berthe used to ask. "Come, let me kiss it better."

Poor Aunt Berthe couldn't have known that nothing could make it better and Natalie couldn't tell her aunt or they would hurt her. They told Natalie they would kill her and anyone she told – the way they had killed her kitten. Although she didn't remember what she wasn't supposed to tell until she heard Aunt Berthe was dead and Bonnie started to draw the horrible pictures. One of Ruthie with a gun. One of Ruthie in a box. Natalie remembers now seeing someone put Ruthie in the box.

Natalie's head is spinning. She clutches at the counter to keep from falling. She might switch now and lose track of what happens. She doesn't want to, she wants to stay present. She's very afraid of going somewhere she doesn't want to go. She suspects that Aunt Berthe's presence acted as a buffer while she was alive because whoever went north stayed with her. She vaguely remembers walking down the main street to the lake, watching horses in a ring near the water go through their paces. All the same, she's afraid she may have done something really horrible even as recently as a month or so ago. She doesn't want to know any more right now.

"I won't go to the funeral," she murmurs. "I don't have to go."

"Aunt Berthe would be glad I'm staying in Toronto to work on my essay," she whispers. "Aunt Berthe wouldn't want anyone to hurt me."

Natalie goes to the bathroom to look for the razor. She finds it behind the toothpaste. She stands in front of the mirror and stares at herself as she begins to cut very lightly on her arm, high up where unless she is wearing a sleeveless blouse the scars won't show. After a few more light slashes she knows will not kill her, or be in a place anyone will ask questions about or require stitches, she sees some blood trickling down her arm. She looks at her face in the mirror again, her expression more relaxed now, and puts the razor back behind the toothpaste.

Who Are You Today?

SUZY BARTRAM'S LEFT KNEE sock slipped down around her ankle as she walked along the street after school. Every day she took a different route, lingering so that she wouldn't have to go home where her mother yelled at her. *Don't mess the living room, clean up those dishes, play outside I'm sleeping.* It was the high, screeching tone that bothered Suzy, as if whatever she did was a nuisance. If she closed the refrigerator door, her mother yelled that she had slammed it. If she ate an apple, it would spoil her supper. After her father came home, it was even worse because they yelled at each other. Suzy hated going home. She often pretended she was someone else's daughter.

"What street is that?" she asked a woman walking by her on the sidewalk, her finger waggling in the direction of a light at the corner, dancing on one foot while she pulled up the sock on the other.

"Where are you going?" the woman asked.

And Suzy could tell from the look in her eyes that she thought Suzy shouldn't be out on her own. Going anywhere. Unless she knew exactly where and even then, even when Suzy told her the House of Gifts Shop, she looked dubious. Little girls were 'ducted, disappeared, their pictures turned up in milk stores with descriptions and no one ever found them. Or sometimes dead children were found, children who had been 'salted, whatever that was. But whatever it was Suzy knew that was what the woman was thinking. She could tell.

"That street will get you there," the woman said.

And before she could ask how old Suzy was or why she was going to the store by herself, Suzy thanked her. "Do you have the time?" she added. "I may be late for work."

The woman frowned as she pushed back her sleeve and looked at her watch. "What kind of work do you do?"

"I'm a cashier." She was about to tell the woman that she had six brothers and sisters and her family was on welfare, but she noticed the guard at the crosswalk was listening. One day he heard her tell someone her mother was in Florida recovering from an operation and that she was looking after her younger brothers. Another time that she lived in an apartment with her grandmother because both her parents were killed in a car accident.

"Oh, you poor thing," the last woman had said, reaching in her handbag for four shiny quarters. "Buy yourself something, dear." As if there was something that four shiny quarters could do about dead parents. It was peculiar the reactions of adults when she told them her stories. You never could predict. Why didn't someone offer to take her home? No one had ever done that.

"Well, Suzy," the crossing guard said. "What are you telling people today?"

She put her nose up in the air and pretended she didn't hear him. Once he told her she could write a bestseller with all the tales she told. Well maybe, but she was going to be an actress, a great actress. So there.

Now he walked out to the middle of the street with his hand raised to stop the traffic. He blew his whistle. Before he came to her corner, there was a small woman with red hair and a kerchief and a sign that looked too heavy for her who helped the children across the street. She had huge glasses that made her eyes bulge and wore the same orange vest the man did. He looked like an orange kangaroo with his feet splaying outwards in his Nike jogging shoes. Suzy crossed the street and stopped at the curb to pull up her knee sock again before she looked around to see if there was anyone else with whom she could carry on a conversation. Maybe she would find a rich person some day who would take her on a trip, someone from that television series, *The Canadian 'Stablishment*. In the first one, there was a fine old house on a street called Victoria, after a queen her mother told her. Maybe she would take the subway downtown. Her mother said the house was there. And she could ask for one of the Black brothers who lived in it. How could people younger than her parents have so much money? If they met her and thought she was like the poor people she saw in a television show on welfare, maybe they would share some with her, or at least take her home for dinner. Her friend, Diana, thought their dentist was rich with his ranch style bungalow in Scarborough, but Suzy would show her.

"Korpration lawyers are rich," she told Diana after she heard her father yell at her mother that he wasn't *a fucking millionaire korpration lawyer* and he could not afford a holiday in Arizona. Or a new car.

"Suzy wants a kitten," her mother said. "That's all I'm asking for. One tiny little kitten."

"Tell the kid to get a paper route."

Suzy wondered what a korpration was, something to do with men in dark suits with white shirts and ties, like a uniform. If she saw someone in a dark suit she would know he was rich, especially if his shoes were polished so that she could almost see her face in them. No one she knew dressed like that. Her father usually wore a tweed jacket and beige shirt and her teacher didn't even wear a tie.

The men Suzy saw on the subway on the way downtown had scuff marks on their shoes. Korpration lawyers probably had those big black shiny cars someone else drove for them. They wouldn't ride underground with children on welfare. She didn't even know what stop to get off at, probably Dundas. She could sit on a bench in the Eaton Centre and watch the people go up and down on the escalators under the geese flying beneath the high ceiling. She had no idea where Victoria Street was. She would have to look it up on her mother's street map and go another day. Unless the man at the ticket booth in the Dundas Station could tell her. If she could find the grey stone house, she might never have to get a paper route. She didn't want to get up early in the morning to deliver *The Globe and Mail*, especially if it were dark and raining. She would tell her father that was the time she really might get 'salted.

There were signs in subway stations that said that you could find all the information you wanted in the library. Maybe they could tell her how to find a korpration lawyer. That was a laugh! The librarian at school might know where the information was, but she sure didn't want anyone else to find it. If you whispered, she barred you from the library that week. Suzy was on her list now and got menacing stares whenever she walked in the door. It was as if Mrs. Schutt wanted to keep all the books for herself. Suzy hoped she didn't have any kids of her own, she made other people's kids so miserable. Probably korpration lawyers had their own libraries for their families. In the grey house on Victoria Street, there would be a room especially for children. Maybe it would be a library. Or maybe a small theatre with a stage where she could practise. When she imitated characters at home, wearing her mother's shoes or a hat of her father's, someone always punished her for leaving a mess or making too much noise. She missed having a brother or sister to talk to, but it was a good thing her parents didn't have more children. Only one drove them crazy.

If she didn't find a rich person today, Suzy decided she would run away anyway. She could go to the waterfront to take a ferry to the island where she could sleep in one of the barns with the animals. Except she would get hungry and she only had two dollars. She should have packed her knapsack. Maybe someone in one of the houses on the far end of the island would let her stay with them. She saw a tall, skinny man on the television news who said the homes should be preserved because it was a community. Her mother said he was the mayor and her father said he was too outspoken.

"Runs down the police," he said.

Suzy thought he sounded like a nice man who wanted to let people stay in their houses. And he didn't run down the police, her mother said. He just wanted to make sure they were fair to everyone.

"He's gay," her father said.

"You're a bigot," her mother replied. "And anyway, he isn't. And if he was, what difference –"

Suzy put her hands over her ears and crawled down under the blanket, afraid they might start yelling at her if she began to whimper. But she wished she could crawl into someone's lap and be stroked and petted. Someone who would never yell at her. She tried to remember the number of the grey house. It wasn't on Victoria Street;

that was another house she learned about in school. She didn't even know the right street so she wouldn't be able to find it on a map. Nor did she know the name of the korpration so she couldn't look it up in the phone book. And there would be too many Blacks for her to figure out anything. It was a common name, her mother said, not like Rockefeller, even if there were a Canadian 'stablishment. Not all lawyers were rich though. Her father's friend, Mr. Wall, was a lawyer, and he wasn't.

"Of course not," Diana said in a superior voice. "He's middle class like us because he's just a legal aid lawyer."

She hated Diana when she used that voice and said words like middle class and legal aid. She wondered where she learned things like that. And what they were in the middle of. Could you be middle class if you started your k'reer selling dew worms as her father's friend, the legal aid lawyer, Mr. Wall, did?

"A fucking entrepreneur at twelve," her father chuckled. He could be jovial when there were other people around. He even put his arm around her mother sometimes then.

Suzy didn't ask Diana what middle class was, but Diana didn't wait to be asked. "You know what I mean," she said. "Middle class is where the father works and the mother gets migraines."

"Lots of mothers have jobs. Most mothers have jobs." If her mother worked, she might be able to afford a kitten. Diana's tabby had another litter and she'd promised one to Suzy.

The train sat in the station at Union and when Suzy realized she'd passed Dundas, she tried to figure out what to do. Maybe it was late enough for her mother to start to worry. She would call Diana first, but Diana wouldn't even guess where she was, right inside Union Station. Her mother said developers wanted to destroy it, but people who wanted to save their history stopped them.

"It's our heritage," her mother said.

"A bunch of yahoos," her father said, although he admitted he liked the building. But he really thought her mother was a yahoo because she picketed the Spadina Expressway and was part of a demonstration at St. Jamestown.

Suzy was too young to remember that, but her mother told her. It was her city they wanted to tear down, her mother said. And she said her father signed all the petitions and spoke at local meetings. Maybe he didn't really hate her mother.

Suzy stood on the platform. Her mother might call the police. Anyway it would be hard to get used to another family, even a rich one. Maybe the Blacks invited the Prime Minister for dinner and would expect her to talk with him at the table. If she said anything about all her father's small dollars, no one would like that very much. Why was it only dollars that had shrunk? Why not quarters? Or ten-dollar bills? The Prime Minister would know, but the Blacks would probably be embarrassed if she asked. They were supposed to know all about money. She would learn more before she tried to find them. Anyway, she was hungry.

When she got to her house, no one noticed she had been gone. Or hardly. "Did you stop to play with someone?" her mother asked. The telephone rang and her mother didn't wait for an answer. And she didn't ask again when she finally finished her conversation.

Suzy went to her room right after she had something to eat and climbed into bed with her rabbit. Not long after, she heard her parents arguing through the wall beside her.

"You're so tight it makes me puke," her mother's voice said. Suzy hugged the big pink rabbit she'd had since she was a baby. She called it Bow-Wow, although she was told often enough that was a stupid name for a rabbit.

"The kid needs to learn the value of money. It doesn't grow on trees," her father shouted.

What did he take her for? Who ever would look for money on trees? Suzy knew it came from machines after you punched enough buttons. You had to know the number and have a card, but that shouldn't be too difficult. She bet none of the korpration lawyers' kids delivered newspapers. And none of their fathers screamed, "*I'm not a fucking millionaire,*" if one of their kids wanted a kitten. Her father could afford a Volvo station wagon, Suzy thought, so he could afford one small kitten. He was just a tightwad with his money. And why did people have children if they hated them? And could even korpration lawyers stay rich if the dollar kept getting smaller? She thought her money looked the same, but she heard her father shout that he couldn't keep up with 'flation. His dollars were only half as big as they were ten years ago and she ought to know half a dollar wouldn't even buy one bag of kitty litter. Poor cat. If they hated kids, they would probably hate a kitten more. It wouldn't be fair to get one just so they could yell at it instead. Except they would probably holler at her anyway, especially if the kitten ever peed on her mother's shiny floors or scratched the furniture. If it got one small scratch on the new chair her mother would probably have hysterics. You would think the chair mattered more to her than her father did. That's what he said anyway when she went over and straightened all the cushions as soon as he stood up. If he smoked cigarettes, she went around emptying ashtrays every time he moved.

"What is this?" he would yell. "A museum? Does every damned ash tray have to be clean all the time?"

Rich people wouldn't yell like that, Suzy thought. Except in meetings if it might make more money.

"Listen," her father said. "She can have the kitten. All I ask is that she does something to learn where money comes from. Is that so unreasonable?"

"I guess not," her mother said. "But don't shout about it if it's not unreasonable."

After that Suzy heard funny kissing noises and her mother start to giggle. There were other noises Suzy didn't understand and she blocked her ears again.

At recess the next day, Suzy played tag with Diana and some boys from another class. After a while, the boys wandered off. Diana had a brother and she told Suzy all about his penis and how he sometimes woke up at night with his sheets wet after groaning in his sleep. Suzy's mother tried to tell her about intercourse once, but Suzy said she already knew that. She saw a film on sex at school. "Cherry glands come and hair starts to grow down there," it said. "Public hair." It was all too gross to think about and especially to talk about with her mother.

"What about the kitten?" Diana asked.

"My father says I can't unless I get a paper route," Suzy said.

"Why?"

"All his money has shrunk."

"What made it shrink?"

"'Flation."

"What's that?"

"I don't know. Probably some detergent, for all I know."

"My father says the government is ruining the country."

"You mean Jimmy Carter."

"He's American."

"He's still government and my father says what he does is more important than anything they do in Ottawa."

That night her father said Black was a smart cookie to get out of Massey-Ferguson. "When he couldn't save it, he jumped ship."

On television, a man asked if helping Massey-Ferguson would help the 'conomy more in the long run than leaving it flounder. Suzy could see the 'conony flapping along in the ocean, some kind of whale or something.

"Either way, it will cost money," the man said.

"They don't do business that way in Japan," her father said.

Her father was pretty smart, Suzy thought. Her mother said he was crabby lately because he didn't get a promotion and he deserved it. He also put some money on something that was moving down because drilling season was over until next year when it might come up again. Maybe her father would have been really sad if she ran away from home. Maybe he didn't hate her either. And if her mother got a job again, she might stop worrying about the floors and the furniture. All of this made Suzy feel immensely better and when she left for school the next morning, she skipped along toward the crossing guard.

"Well, Suzy," the crossing guard said. "Who are you today?"

Suzy wrinkled her nose at him as she crossed the street. She saw a woman with a stroller just ahead of her. When she caught up with her, she looked down at the baby. He gurgled and grinned at her and waved his fist back and forth.

"He's really cute," she said to the woman. "If you'd like, I'll give you a dollar to buy something for him. My father says his dollars have all shrunk, but this one's all right because it's the same size as it used to be."

"It's all right, dear," the woman said. "I think we can manage."

"I have a little brother his age," Suzy said. "The governess looks after him while my mother runs one of my father's korprations. My name is Black and my father's a korpration lawyer and korpration lawyers are very rich, you know."

The Yellow Volvo

EVA WRAPS TWO PLATES in newspaper and puts them in a cardboard box. She finds mugs and wraps them in newspaper also, old copies of the *Toronto Star* ready to be recycled. Although she's spent almost thirty years with Bill, he has no idea what she's doing. She's sure he won't even notice anything is gone because there are so many plates and saucers piled on shelves and in cupboards. All the debris from garage sales and construction sites that he brings home to repair and sell, but never touches again. He won't discard anything, even though there are now six television sets that don't work in the dining room and nine toasters and a dozen fans spread throughout the house. The clutter is unbearable.

As she packs some glasses carefully in the classifieds, Eva is terrified he might come in unexpectedly. This is something she has been doing only when he's not around. Once she has taken everything she wants to the apartment near Bloor and Spadina, she doesn't intend to return. She knows why as clearly as if it were written on a billboard high above the city. Although there was a time when she first knew him that he treated her well. Bought her flowers. Told her she was beautiful. She knew she wasn't all that attractive, nowhere near as beautiful as her best friend at the time, Lena, but she'd liked his flattery.

Not long after they were married, Bill began to taunt her, and then push her around. It slowly dawned on her that he was both a bully and a coward. Pregnant with their first child, it didn't occur to her there was anything she could do about it. Not only that, but he always had guns around, knives, even an axe. One night, Eva dreamed that she found the bodies of three women chopped in pieces and tied up in packages dripping with blood in a refrigerator in the kitchen. In the dream, there were five refrigerators. The packages were in the one that didn't work and had begun to smell. Eva awakened with a sore back and tight shoulders.

She never told anyone what went on behind the doors and windows of their messy house. Except finally Lena who turned up one day from Windsor, as if there weren't thirty years in between, and invited her to lunch at Fran's. Lena questioned her until she finally admitted she was frightened. Fed up with the shouting. The put-downs. The occasional shoves. Although he never hit her, she said, or even threatened to. But she has seen him throw a toaster through a window and has withered at his shouts when he's angry. Now Lena will help her move the remainder of her clothes and books out on the weekend when Bill is in San Francisco for a meeting, something about the financial implications for his clients of some new technology. He'll be gone a week.

As soon as Eva is settled into her apartment with windows overlooking a larger building next door, but with a view of the street through the space between the high rise and her own place, she packs a bag to go to visit a cousin. She doesn't want to be in the city when Bill returns. The children are grown up and living in far flung places – St. John's, Montreal, and Flin Flon. They don't want any part of the crowded house she lives in with Bill. They've listened to enough of the incessant scorn their father metes out in a sarcastic, belligerent tone. They told her years ago it was all right with them if she left him. Some day soon, probably while at her cousin's, she'll sit down and write to each of them.

Dear Margie ... I know this won't come as a surprise to you, but I wanted to tell you as soon as possible so you wouldn't worry if ... Dear Gordon ... I know this ... Dear Katherine.

Eva does write the letters, but they are still on the front seat of the car as she drives back to Toronto. Neatly addressed, without stamps yet. She'll mail them the next day. Or the day after. After she has let Bill know she won't be coming back. At first she thought she would leave a note, but at the last minute she decided not to. She'll call him.

As she drives along the 401 past Oshawa, Eva decides to make the call from a phone booth at the next rest stop. If she calls ahead, he'll have calmed down by the time she reaches her apartment. Although he doesn't know where she has moved and she doesn't intend to tell him, she still figures she would feel the impact of his anger more directly were she actually in her new apartment.

The station she finds is a Petro Canada, she can see the ad on television with the boy with reddish hair talking to customers through a car window. A friendly place, Petro Canada. There's a yellow Volvo at the gas pumps.

When she dials the familiar number, good heavens, they've lived in the same house for almost all of the thirty years they've been married, her hands are trembling. Cars whiz by on the highway, spewing water on the windshields behind them. Eva can see Lake Ontario and the bluffs through the light rainfall. When she was a child, she used to visit her grandparents in a house above the lake that looked out over the blue water. Often she watched the white sails in summer. She called them tepees and pretended she was sailing away into the distance to a place where her mother would never again push her into a corner and scream at her, "*What a horrible girl you are. You've wrecked my life.*"

There was also a farm on the flat part down below where she picked cherries. Now the land has eroded and there's only water. And her mother lives in a house that is filthy. Except when Eva goes to clean it. Meals on wheels bring food five times a week, but her mother shoves most of it under her bed. Next month she'll go into a nursing home. One more small victory for Eva.

As she listens to the dial tone, Eva thinks of the white sails on Lake Ontario and that she's finally at the rudder of one of them. She thinks of cherry trees in blossom and later of picking the dark red berries from the lower branches and eating them. She watches the family in the yellow Volvo climb over each other to get out and dash around the gas station. A teenage boy in blue jeans with a hole in the knee and a patch on the left cheek of his bottom pushes ahead of a younger brother to get into the washroom. The younger one begins to shriek and the mother dashes across and waits with him in the rain. She wears a red plastic raincoat and big black rubber boots with thick soles. She holds a black umbrella over their heads. The man comes out of the restaurant with a bag of donuts and two other children circle around him.

"Now," one of them says. "I want one now."

She wants the chocolate one with coconut on it. The boy in the washroom emerges and asks for the apple fritter.

"It's the biggest," he says.

Eva longs to be part of a family like this one. She imagines how they talk in the car. They count cows, they remark on out-of-province license plates. They play word games and win prizes for long sentences. And long silences. The donuts are prizes. That her own children have never had such a family rankles her. There's nothing she can do now to change that, but she'll mail the letters to let them know she's finally done what they've all said she should do. It has taken almost thirty years to decide to and six months longer to find and move into the apartment.

There are five rings during which her heart beats so hard she thinks she might vomit. Then Bill picks up the receiver. His voice booms into it, as if his whole body is poised to jump into the telephone. She can feel her words stop in her throat and she's about to hang up when the man from the yellow Volvo hugs the woman in the red rain slicker. They watch as the last child piles into the rear of the car and then grin at each other. Eva has a lump in her throat.

"Bill, it's Eva," she says, blinking back tears.

"Where are you?"

"At a pay phone."

"Where's my dinner? I told you when my flight was arriving. Didn't you even call to check it out?" he snarls.

"I've called to tell you I won't be coming back, Bill." She stops, expecting a loud blast through the earpiece, but he is suddenly quiet, doesn't say anything, instead breathes heavily into the phone. She is trembling as she stands in the booth with the door broken off behind her, waiting. "I have an apartment and I'm on my way there now," she says.

That night she will dream that she's standing on the street in a crowd of people milling around the doors of the Bloor Cinema and that she flaps her arms and is suddenly propelled upwards. She floats above the people, the streets, the buildings, and out over some fields with patches of snow on them. When she awakens, she'll keep flapping her arms for the first few minutes.

The yellow Volvo blinks a turn signal and moves out onto the highway. It disappears into the ribbon of cars moving west towards Toronto. The teenager with the patch on the seat of his jeans is driving. The man sits in the back with the other children. Eva remembers the most recent letter from her son in Flin Flon. He's the youngest, still unmarried. When he comes to the city for a visit, she's surprised at his unruly hair and the swagger in his walk. Surprised, but not unhappy. Nothing has squelched his spirit. Nor that of the other two, for that matter. Now it's her turn. She should hang up before Bill says anything, but she's curious now. What he is about to say might undermine or demean her, but it won't stop her.

He snorts and she can imagine his nostrils flaring and his face so contorted that it looks like an angry pig's. But then the face becomes quiet, determined, or so she imagines, as it does at the chess games set up around the house, all at different stages in their progress. He sits down and thinks for a few moments and then he moves a bishop or pawn or something.

"There," he says with relish. "There."

Next time it will be "Check." After that? There's something menacing about all these games against invisible opponents, something Machiavellian, beyond her comprehension. Or even her desire to comprehend. When he still doesn't speak, Eva continues to wait, the palm of her hand damp against the receiver. She knows when he does speak, his words will be measured, almost as if he's been rehearsing them for weeks or months or years, as if he's always known what he would say if this moment came. But this time she's not going to let him get to her.

"I always wondered what took you so long," he says.

Eva shudders, pursing her lips. She decides to say nothing, instead looks at the receiver and hangs it up. And after standing there for a minute, she strides across the pavement to the restaurant.

"I'd like a chocolate donut with coconut on it," she says. "And an apple fritter."

From the Front

7:30 A.M.

WALK AWAY from the house, looking back once at the cat with its nose pressed against the glass. Used to watch for the children coming home from school from that window. Children used to wait for me there when I came back from a shift. Often I rode my bicycle to the office of the crisis line. Now the sun is shining and there is only an occasional cloud in the sky. I can hear the whine of a streetcar on tracks a block away. The world feels momentarily normal, not full of menace.

Welcome day!

8:30 a.m.

Open the line after night shift person leaves.

Woman in flashback. O.J. Simpson trial as trigger. Still triggered by Bernardo. Bodies found in ditches. Remembers being encased in trunk or chest as small child. No food. Given feces. Made to perform fellatio. Gradually responds to my voice saying it wasn't her fault, asking her if she's standing, lying down, sitting. She's in her room. The walls are pale peach. She has a painting of a waterfall done by a friend on the wall. Her cat is beside her, long white fur, pink nose with a dark splotch. Fat Cat. It is 1995. Yes, she says. 1995. Maybe she can put the razor (pills, knife, gun?) away now. Can she? Yes. Skinny Cat died. She still misses him. But Fat Cat is with her. She'll eat some breakfast, walk to the corner.

Long call.

9:25 a.m.

Glass of water. Next call.

He's gone to work, but he checks up on her. She can't take it any more. Last night he tried to choke her. She didn't call the police because he pulled the phone out of the wall last time she tried to. He held her down. He says if she ever calls the police he'll kill her, if she leaves he'll find her and kill her. She has two young children. She's afraid to stay and afraid to leave. She's sure if she either calls the police or leaves, he will kill her. He hasn't yet when she stays, maybe that's safer. After a while, she begins to think she might go to a shelter.

All the shelters are full. Finally find space at Family Res. *Another long call.*

10:15 a.m.

Pee break. Another glass of water. Next call. A hang up. A few minutes later, someone wants to make a donation of women's and children's clothing to a shelter.

After that a low voice struggling with English. She isn't yet landed. He threatens to have her deported. He has another woman and goes back and forth. He has children with both of them. *Struggle to make out what she's saying. Enough English to manage.* He's started to beat her. She doesn't want to call the police. She comes from a country where the police are part of the problem. You can't be sure they'll lay charges either. You tell her they're supposed to, that what's happening is a crime here. No, she doesn't want the cops, that's clear. Shelter? She has some relatives, she might go there. She takes the number of a service where her language is spoken. *Didn't access interpreter service, over 150 languages available in less than a minute for a conference call.*

Feel angry, time for a break. Phone ringing.

10:50 a.m.

I'm having a little problem with my husband. *That's what she says. That's how calls often start. A little problem. With her husband or her boyfriend. If it's a girlfriend, it's usually less direct, it takes the woman longer to say so. Either way, it takes a while to get to the whole picture of what is going on.* No, he doesn't hit her, he just pushes her around a little. Although there was that one time a month or so ago when he tried to strangle her with the telephone cord. One of the kids was watching. Age three. A girl. The boy was just a baby then. He was sleeping. Although he started to scream, too.

He doesn't give her any money. She doesn't know how she's going to buy food, clothes. He says she doesn't work hard enough, the kids aren't clean enough, the apartment. She doesn't deserve the money. He tells her she's a slut, a whore, a bitch, in front of the children. But no one would ever believe it. Everyone thinks he's a golden-haired angel. He treats everyone else so well, they think she's crazy. And he's a good father, she says. She doesn't want to call the cops, he's a police officer.

Oh my God. Out into the large room wanting to scream. There's a meeting. Out into the hall. Down to the bathroom. We need those little bags airlines put in the pockets in front of passengers to throw up in.

It's not her fault. He isn't taking responsibility for....

How do they get off with blaming her all the time?

Time for a break whether there's a line open or not, else will scream. Where does he think he gets the right to take a telephone cord and strangle her? Where do these guys get the idea they can do whatever they want. Some God given right that men think they have. A cop? It's not the first time there's been a call like this. Nor the second or third. It makes you almost puke. At the system. Women aren't people, they're a special interest. Property, too, still.

Maybe it's time to quit this kind of work.

Pee. Walk out to the street. Look up at the sky. See the CN Tower in the distance. Can see it from almost every vantage point in this city. Wires across the sky, too, everywhere you look. A streetcar. A man and woman having a friendly conversation. A child laughing. A bird. Deep breath. No big trucks or buses to create fumes going by at this moment. Sigh. One more call, possibly two or three, and it will be lunch time.

11:50 a.m.

The phone doesn't ring. Other counsellors on the lines. A memo on the desk from the new director. Important to go to staff meetings. Personnel policy # 10.5(a). Funding cuts imminent. Clean off the top of your desk when finishing your shift. Doesn't mention sunflower seeds on the floor or dirty dishes in the sink. Wants feedback on work environment. Do you get support from your colleagues? Staff supervisor? Administrator? Family and friends? Do you feel valued? What do you think of the space? PLEASE PRINT.

Hello, this is...

His wife was harassed at work by her boss, he made lewd comments, he tried to entice her into some kind of sexual involvement. Now she's been fired on some pretext so she can't complain. He's irate and he's driving his car on the Gardiner Expressway. *Oh my, give him some information fast before he cuts someone off and ends up dead on a guardrail. Hate idiots who talk on their cell phones in the midst of traffic.*

He calms down a little when he hears level tone. A lousy situation. There are places she can complain. *Not sure what good it will do, but hey, you tell him anyway.* Tell him she can also call here. He says he'll tell her.

Look down at memo. What anyone thinks of space doesn't really matter if there's no money, if there are no lines to take these calls, if ...

Get support from some colleagues, think space is adequate, but tired of sound of construction coming from floor above. Too much noise and dust and no cooperation from building management. Wore a mask to work once when plaster dust was so thick it coated all the furniture. Maybe time to move again. Except will miss going to Kensington Market on lunch break to pick up fruit and vegetables. Great cheese, too.

12:16 p.m.

Caller is a social worker at a hospital. Has a friend who is afraid to go home. If it were a client, she says she'd know what to do. Turns out it's her sister. Can't convince her sister to leave or call the police or do anything and she's terrified she'll get killed.

She's always been a strong person and now she's with this jerk who uses her money to buy drugs. He may even be a drug dealer and things are getting worse.

Turns out caller is the older sister, the one the whole family has always turned to, thinks she has to fix it.

Whew! Used to be like that. Ms. Fixit. Brother called from San Diego after the subway crash. Wondered if I was all right. Doesn't know much else about my life except I wasn't on the subway the night one train crashed into another and three people were killed. Terrible. Never happened before in Toronto. Safety record for years. Gone now. Won't ride that leg of the subway for a while. Won't sit in front or back car of train. Thanks for calling, brother. Still doesn't know what my life is like on a daily basis. Kids gone now. Not only from home, but from city. Dinner with niece last night, eggplant parmigian. Not much cheese, lots of eggplant and thick tomato sauce with cayenne, chili, red peppers, carrots. Delicious. Crepes with apple filling for dessert. Walked on the Danforth. A caller last week had purse stolen on Danforth.

Okay, social worker says. Can suggest sister call, can offer place for her to stay, can let her know she doesn't have to put up with it, that she can call police. Thanks for listening.

You're welcome.

Write up call, ticks for statistics. Relative/friend of abused woman. Abuser is male. Married/common law/partner ... that circle. Crisis issues identified. Support given. Time of call. Length of call. Information for funders, for advocacy, for internal changes. Is it time for lunch yet? No. Not quite. The whole world treads on my dreams. Bruises and batters them. Hers. Her sister's. Every woman's. Now it's going to be lower welfare rates and more visits to food banks.

1:00 p.m.

One more short call. Then lunch. Short call goes on for forty-five minutes. At first the caller thanks her, says she's called before and it was very helpful. Could record this as gratitude. Don't remember her, probably talked to another counsellor. Then woman starts into most recent episode of being pushed by her ex when he came to pick up one of their children and ... Fooled on that one. Know it will go on after first few sentences. Don't make any plans with anyone else when on the front. Always get changed by whatever crisis comes up at the moment. Get right into call. Lose world around. Relieved when it's over and can slip out and walk in the sunshine, can move through the small shops below College, bright green peppers, red, yellow, squash at this time of year, lots of fresh apples, pears. Listen to lilting voices, step over puddle in street, screw up nose going past fish store. Down to Dundas and back again. Walk fast, walk slow, breathe, remember sister called from west coast after subway crash also. But she knows about rest of life, maybe not about lonely, but more of the other things, from before, before I finally left. Walked and sketched with her on last holiday out there. Thought Mum would have enjoyed comradeship of her daughters. Except then she'd add, "Too bad brother isn't there, too." Always some small note of dissatisfaction. Still, miss her at times.

2:30 p.m.

Woman starts slowly. She's not in an abusive relationship any more. Stuck in small basement apartment. Wants to move, but doesn't have enough money for first and last. Sometimes feels suicidal. Father killed self when she was a child. One day two women turned up and mother got suitcase out from behind couch, already packed, and let women take her. Never warned her. Just let her go. Into foster homes. In the first one, a boy sexually abused her. In the next home, the father. No one ever believed her. She got moved because she screamed and yelled and stole something from a corner grocery store. Seven foster homes before the group ones. Saw her mother once as an adult, went to ask why. No answers. No connection. She doesn't care what happens to her mother. She hates her.

Makes you wonder how some people could ever turn their lives around. Encourage her to find therapist. Thanks for listening, she says. Might be enough to get her through one day.

3:15 p.m.

Quick pee break. Toilets are dirty. Must be day cleaner comes in, hope so. Never seems to see the walls of the stalls. Same marks for months now. Better not to wear glasses into the washroom, can't see then. Civil servants wouldn't work in these offices. Government gets good bang for its buck, but they're going to cut funding anyway. Helter skelter. Compassionate society down the tube?

3:20 p.m.
   Hang up.
   Another call. Woman says sorry she hung up the first time, wasn't ready to talk or thought maybe it would be useless. Doesn't have the energy any more to do anything. Too worn down by the putdowns, the threats. Everything her fault. *Always thought it was all my fault, too. Took so long to believe otherwise. To leave. Hard for the children, but never tried to prevent them from loving him.*

4:00 p.m.
   Check answering machine at home. Vegetarian Association announcing a dinner. Annual meeting. Second message, dinner at Chinese restaurant on Spadina with group of friends who do other kinds of work. Too tired after today's calls. Some other time. Third message, call and tell matriarch, contemporary of parents, if can go for snacks and drinks. She's trying to get all the "children" together. Only person calls me a child any more. All the "children" she's trying to reach are over fifty. When reach her, she says, well, what else would she call us?
   Open line. Feel better. Rings. Counsellor at other desk slams the window. Must have had an especially tough call. After a walk, she'll be okay. Will try to notice if she needs to talk when she comes back.
   I'm having a little problem with … *Oh jeez, sounds familiar, doesn't it? Too familiar. Oh jeez.*

4:45 p.m.
   Close the line. Someone coming in to replace me in other room. Service still available, anonymous, confidential, 24/7. Go home to see own cat. Not Fat Cat or Skinny Cat. Call black one with white paws and white around nose Mr. Boots, Esquire. Mister, for short. Don't hate men. Just don't like what some of them do. And want my tax money to support a just and compassionate society, but can't get through to the big guys who make

the rules. The big guys who think it's important to give someone earning $95,000 a tax break.

5:30 p.m.

Sun still shines, neighbour waves from across the street, children play in front yard of another house.

"Did you have a good day?" neighbour calls.

I nod. It was fine. Not something to talk about. "Your garden is lovely," I say.

Soon will play music, cook simple meal, read mail. Approach front door, see cat in window. Turn knob. Reach for letters poking out of box.

Cat purrs and winds around my legs.

"Hello, Mister."

Time to shut blinds, turn on radio, start heating some leftover minestrone soup, ignore ringing of the telephone.

First She Killed Him

YES, SHE DID. *FIRST SHE KILLED HIM!* Yet Rosemary (better known to herself and some friends as "Roseberry") had not been quite sure whom she had in reality killed. So she went to the funeral parlour. And even then she was not sure, just went because every day people died (or were killed?) and it did not seem appropriate somehow that she should escape that part of having been involved in the death. Going to jail seemed highly inappropriate, in fact had not even crossed her mind. But why should she escape the funeral parlour?

She was supposed to be at a party, a family party. Rosemary thought she might not feel up to it after seeing the body though. But her family did not know about the murder. Or anything else about her life, her secret life, that had gone on all around them ever since she could remember, but they NEVER knew. But because it was a special occasion (the party, not the murder, in fact she thought it might be her birthday) they "rather hope you will come, Rose." (No, someone else's birthday.) After all, you never come, Rose. Never come. What will people think? No. No. They rarely said that any more. Not since the murder they did not know about. That other refrain they had used when she was a child of thirty-two or twenty-seven or eight and eighteen before she became thirty-five or forty-two or ... And killed him. Before their party. "You always were thoughtless, Rose." But she was NOT thoughtless. She was ALWAYS thinking. Maybe THEY were thoughtless. Although, she supposed, they would have an answer for that.

"*Rosemary, dear*, that's not very polite." Well, wasn't it polite of her to go to the funeral parlour?

"Yes, ma'am," a quiet, discreet man said to her as she walked across the red, plush carpet, along the quiet hall hesitantly. "Which...?"

And then she realized she was not following her mind searching for a clue to whom she might be looking for because she did not know his name. And did not want to. And would they guess and block her from entering one of these rooms, any of these rooms, from which quiet whispers emanated?

It's all right, she assured them with a nod. Her everyday nod. After all, she thought, it really doesn't matter what body. She could have killed anyone. But no. No. You must understand. She wouldn't have killed JUST anyone. Not a child. Not anyone who did not really threaten her mind. A child had never done that. Threatened to crawl into it and expose it or ridicule it or… You could walk up to children on the street and ask what day it was and when they said Thursday, you could say what month, and they'd tell you without even thinking the question was peculiar or you were absurd.

"The man," she said to the discreet gentleman still accompanying her, ready to guide her ever so gently… "The grey…" Surely there would be a dead man with grey hair. In a city this large, in a funeral home this large, there must be a dead man each day with grey hair.

"Ah, yes," he said soothingly. Very well mannered! Very well trained! Very well groomed! Very well paid. "Just down the hall, the third door to the left."

Rosemary walked down the plush carpet that her bare feet sank into (she looked down and found she was wearing shoes, her quite ordinary brown shoes, but she still felt the carpet brushing sensually against her bare feet) and peered into the room behind the curtain held back by a very discreet chain. She was glad for a moment that he was going to have a proper funeral. A polite funeral.

Just inside the door there was a man standing with his hands behind his back. The son? The brother? The old friend? The nephew? Oh, it did not matter. She clasped his hand as he thrust it forward. And then held him. Held him until they were lying together on the carpet, the soft, plush carpet, but no one noticed. No one noticed. She murmured words of condolence to him. "We'll all miss him, too." But suddenly she meant it and standing shaking the hand of this strange man, big tears caught in her throat.

And then, did he take it well? she wondered. Being killed.·

"He was brave until the end. And then his heart..."

And then his heart? But she thought she had murdered him. This was the wrong room. No, this was the right room. She had moved to the open coffin. And there was a man's body with grey hair. And even in his pale, still whiteness Rosemary could see a man alive. Or a man living, a variation of features falling into focus in her mind. And he was, or could have been, the character she had stolen from the next door cottage on vacation last summer on another lake they had rented. She always took over the whole lake, or whatever, when she went somewhere. And she had stolen this man. And then drowned him.

"I learned so much from him," she whispered to the son. He must be the son. Except that for a moment the corpse looked like his twin, not his father. She frowned and felt out of place suddenly. But she was glad she had come to his funeral even though, as it happened, she had not really killed him. He had just died. And she said to the young man, "There are worse things than dying." After all. Killing. Although maybe not all the lesser misdemeanours she probably committed endlessly without ever having to account for them.

He looked puzzled as he agreed. And he would have asked her how she knew his father, but it seemed an intrusion on her privacy. On her grief? But then he said, "How did you know him?"

Oh, no one was even going to tell her his name. How frightful. Now she would have to spin the truth into something he could believe or a lie into the truth and she never knew which worked best and hurt least. Sometimes it was one, sometimes the other. Although usually people believed the lies more readily and rejected the truth so she just started to tell him nervously what came to her mind and whether it was true or false, she even believed it herself now, only wondered at how mad he would think her. She wished he were a child on the street. Who would have understood. "Well, you see, I found him one summer fishing in a boat and I watched him and watched him. And said 'good morning,' of course. Everyone says 'good morning' when you rent a lake. And they wave from big boats with little flags on them as they zoom by and their waves scare all your fish away. But he wasn't like that. He said 'good morning' and meant it and he slowed down when he came in close to your line or saw children swimming. He loved that lake, didn't he! I used to watch him explore it and he knew when a storm was coming up before I heard the first thunder, always arrived back on time. And I watched him. Just because I was sitting there. And it was my lake for that day, too, or those days. And ONE DAY, I woke up in his head. And I looked out of my eyes and saw everything from inside HIS head. Even me. Sitting there on the shore with a sunburn and a funny red hat I wore that summer. And I was thinking his thoughts. DO YOU KNOW? You know…" No, how would he know?

"I see. I see. How utterly fascinating. Except," he said slowly and with a puzzled frown. "Except he hated fishing. He never went fishing in his life." He (his name was Hank or Henry, it varied, today almost everyone called him Henry) wondered if she sat somewhere during most of her days, somewhere she must have escaped from? And created these psychotic fantasies and fictions while people brought her … brought her what? Bread and water?

"Well, maybe he was the one I saw in the park. Feeding the pigeons," she said. "You probably won't understand but it doesn't matter. Maybe I should ask you. How did you know him?"

He jumped slightly. He could ask to have her removed. He could. He could do anything he wanted since it was his father who was dead and people were letting him take all the initiatives. He could even cry. Yes, father, I could even cry. Unmanly though it might seem to that corpse who might just sit up and say "HENRY" in an imperious voice, one last gesture of authority before the lid was closed on him forever. How did he know him? Did he know him at all? "That's a puzzle," he said. "Not very well. Although I've known him for years. I never got into his head at all," and he bit off his words suddenly. If he continued, she would soon begin to think his paradoxes obscene or insane or…

And suddenly she was not frightened of him, as she once had

been. The last time. And she did not think he knew everything and she knew nothing, as she had thought then. Whenever that was. But she knew it was sometime. And Rosemary began to think if she knew that, then she might not hurt him. As murder hurts anyone, of course, whatever kind of murder ... And so, although she wasn't intending, in spite of her insatiable curiosity, to ask any more questions and least of all anyone's name, she suddenly said, "Do you have a name?"

"Hank Hagerty," he said, although he was a little wary of telling her, but he felt peculiarly safer in this funeral parlour where he sensed some humour and warmth she had lacked the last time. The last time? And he thought he would just grab her hand and they would fly from this place like Mary Poppins, just drift across the relatives and the coffin and go wherever they wanted and start from the beginning, having already arrived at where they were and then encountering each other. Oh, no, that would be too simple. He would have to recover from this mad world gone dream, this mad dream gone real on him. Reel. Reeling reel. Real reel. And then –

Hag Hagerty? Hag? No. "Hello, Hank. You're his son then." That was peculiar, Rosemary thought. To know that. Well, perhaps not. She remembered now only that he had the same nose as the man in the casket. And her own intuition that some noses were very revealing. Sometimes. This was an intelligent nose. She liked that kind of nose.

"Yes," Hank said. But she knew that, he thought. This mad dream gone real, this –

"I wondered... Do you have a mother?" Rosemary asked.

"You mean you haven't seen my mother? She'll never forgive me if she doesn't see you. You knew her well, too. Of course."

"Yes, of course," Rosemary said, wondering which one was his mother. Oh, yes, that small, white bird sitting there. Small, frail, and rigidly independent. Who had been slated to perform the murder for Rosemary. Rosemary-berry, the coward. And now. Now, what would she say to her? What would Rosemary-berry say to her? That murder was after all too predictable? Or trite? (How could murder be trite?) But, for whatever reason, Rosie had let her get away with rejecting it, but not without thinking it, not without deciding to let him drown and then deciding not to, being suitably contrite, upset and fearful. Because he was going to die anyway? Although our Rosemary, the weaver of real reels of fantasies and fictions had not known that. Or at least not that it would happen so soon. After all, everyone died anyway. Sooner or later. But that hadn't been why. She had suddenly felt he did not deserve it, that although when they looked at each other next nothing would be very different, he deserved it no more than she did. An ordinary life. And an ordinary death. It was all, she, Rosemary, would ask. So she gave them back their ordinary lives. Yes, I gave them back to you. And did you go on mucking them up? Oh, she sighed, there must be some compassion in her that would provide her with the words that might reach this sad, small woman. And soon. Because there was a small procession heading towards Hank's mother now.

But all Rosemary could say was, "We'll miss him, too."

"These things happen," Hank's mother said.

"These things happen," she said to the next person in line.

"These things happen," she said.

Rose knew a bird in a cage in a pet store on a street in Vancouver that could talk, but he (she?) only said about five things. "Close the door." "I am a talking bird."

"These things happen," Hank's mother said.

"These things happen," she said.

Do these things happen? That this was NOT Hank's mother. That this woman was from another story and had not been the woman of some small insight at all. The woman who had at least been able to draw some thoughts together in her mind after the dreadful experience of thinking of murder, and then after the dreadful experience of being afraid her husband had drowned anyway. Who could ever straighten it out? Hank, she's not your mother. If he's your father, she's not your mother. No, better not tell him.

These things happen...

Then it was nine and everybody left. The discreet man came and accompanied them all out to their cars, their black cars (no, those came tomorrow when they would go through all the red traffic lights with their headlights on and follow the procession) where Uncle Charlie insisted upon taking Hank's mother (he had a nose like a bird's, he must be her brother) home for the night.

As Roseberry-Mary left the funeral parlour she moved quietly in the background. Hank approached her as Uncle Charles drove away in his solid green Buick.

"Thank you for coming."

She nodded.

"Are you still hungry?"

She nodded. She was a nodding bird.

"And tired," he said.

"Yes," she said.

"And a writer."

"Yes." And now, after everything, and knowing he knew, she really was tired. To have killed or not to have killed. Was that ever the question? Should that ever be a question? But to have killed or to have been killed? Supposing that was the question. And if it was, then what?

"I knew a writer once," Hank said. "She was terribly wound up with the notion. It was to be quite an undertaking. To make people aware of Canada. She was applying for a grant."

"Of course," Rose muttered. Self-defence would help the case for either party. Possibly along with temporary insanity.

"...And thought she should go to the publisher with an outline. The writing would be easy. All she would have to do was sit down and write and later pare away the adjectives."

These things happen, Rosemary thought. These things happen. "Writing is a crazy way to stay sane," she said. "I wonder what happened to her."

"Oh, she's not writing. She's still talking," Hank said. "What happened to you?"

"Who, me? Oh, I got the forms," Roseberry said. And a car honked at them as they crossed a street.

"What forms?"

"For the grant. And they asked where *she* served her apprenticeship, who could vouch for *her* work. And *she* looked woefully at the wastebasket. 'Dear Sir: There it is. My apprenticeship. In the wastebasket. Every day...' Then I ripped them up and added them to my wastebasket. Oh, let's forget it, let's go to a party. I have to go to a party. A family ritual. I've seen your family. Now ... would you come to my party? It might even be my birthday. I forget. And I won't tell them we've had a day of 'functions'. I lead a private life. In any case, *en tous cas, ils vont dire*, 'crude, rude, insensitive Rose. Never changes.'"

"All right," he said. His mother wouldn't notice he was gone, was not in the green Buick. She never noticed very much. His father noticed everything, but he was dead. Or maybe it was the other way around. How could you ever be sure?

"Besides," she said. "They give me all the filler."

"Filler?"

"Have you ever made a cushion? You take a shell, or a form, and stuff it. You'll see." You'll see why I almost murdered your father, she thought. He had changed since the last time. He would see.

"How old are you now, Hank?" but he did not answer. She was impertinent, irreverent, and anyway he had forgotten.

When they arrived at the party, the lights were all blazing. And as they walked into the decorated basement recreation room the voices began, "Rosie, Rosie, Rosie Mary. Happy birthday. We thought you'd never come. Everybody, look, it's our Rose. And she brought a friend. Who's your friend, Rose?"

"Hank Hagerty," she said.

And they began to surround and swallow Hank, too, especially the women. She hoped he would escape alive from their reminiscences because she could already hear the old stories beginning. Dan and Roderick who drank all evening and stayed polite (Roseberry was always at home with the sitter visualizing the bizarre shape of two drunk, polite men. Filler, she thought now. Filler. Would they brand her a criminal if they knew how she stole and distorted their memories?)

"Polite," Hank murmured. "Polite? How extraordinary."

The thing is, Hank, Roseberry thought, they could do ANYTHING as long as they were polite about it.

And then on the way home Roderick always went off the slippery roads (parties in the north were always in the winter, but once it had snowed in July so maybe summer was only a chimera somewhere between the end of one winter and the beginning of another) and his wife, Doreen, was always prepared. She had her "woollies" on and blankets ready to drape around them. Prepared to sit in the ditch. And never complained afterwards to anyone, only said, "The roads were dreadful," although everyone knew Roderick was a dreadful driver and roaring (politely) drunk to boot. And now, Roseberry thought, Roderick is dead. Ohmigod, do you suppose it was him, in the casket? No. No ... Because Doreen is in a mental institution or rest home as they call them now. She's not with Hank's Uncle Charlie. Maybe she is sitting there in the rest home in her woollies, covered with a plaid blanket, saying...

"These things happen."

"These things happen."

"These things happen."

And Rosemary's family and friends laughed. THEY LAUGHED! And sang, "Happy birthday, Rosie Mary, Mary Rose. Happy birthday to you." And they brought out a chocolate chip cookie with one candle and handed it to her. "Make a wish, make a wish," they chanted. So she wished she could eat the cookie, but after she blew out the candle they took the cookie away.

Maybe Doreen had also sat in the car in the ditch saying, "These things happen, these things happen."

Then someone started to tell the story about Lorne Petrie's grandfather because everyone was laughing and when everyone was laughing someone always told that story. Rosemary looked for Hank. She must get him out of here so he would not have to hear how Lorne's grandfather died right in the middle of the party season (which began around mid-December and lasted until the undecorated trees with the odd straggling strand of tinsel turned up in the snowbanks in January) and Lorne's mother had to travel by train in the passenger section with the corpse in a freight car at the front of the train because grandfather had only been visiting, had a plot in a small town four hundred miles away. And Mrs. Petrie and the casket made all the transfers and changes to get from their dot on the map to that other one down south somewhere in the Ottawa valley. They travelled and travelled and travelled. As Rosemary remembered it they went on travelling forever. Overnight. To the funeral parlour in the town near the plot in the Ottawa valley (there would not have been plush carpets, Rosemary thought, more likely sawdust on the floor) where the undertaker solemnly opened the casket and Mrs. Petrie's hand flew up to her mouth and her eyes registered her shock.

"But ... ah ... but ... but that isn't my father," Mrs. Petrie was reported to have said. Laugh. Everybody laugh. This is a party. It's Rosemary's birthday party and we're telling funny stories to amuse Rose and her friend, the friend she brought from somewhere to celebrate her birthday.

Still, Rosemary could have assured Hank that they would have handled the body politely, even the wrong one. Even with good humour. Ignoring all the grotesque possibilities. Never contemplating or suspecting murder for one instant, not even an instant. Supposing, for instance, Rosemary thought, the possibility of a criminal in the freight car who had disposed of Lorne Petrie's grandfather and put another body in the casket hoping no one would ever check. And just throwing poor Gramp into the snow drifts from the fast-moving train. But no. They would just send, had sent, telegrams to Englehart, Swastika, Petawawa, God knows where else, until they discovered the mix-up and exchanged bodies. It took a little longer. That was all.

"Hank, do they have any idea of the violence?" Roseberry whispered, catching the frenzied look in Hank's eyes, and before she remembered that he might suspect she had killed his father, and that it might just as well have been him. Until recently.

"Pardon?" he said.

"It's all right," she said soothingly. It was over. She was finished with murder.

146

But Roseberry's mother had heard and looked somewhat disturbed. "Rose*mary*, dear," she said. "Politeness is our standard still. It was our generation. At least those who came after know what we stood for and what we rejected. You'll do the same," she said. "The standards may be different, but you'll have some."

Roseberry was speechless. What could she say? These people were safe somehow. Protected. Even on the icy roads where all the cars went in the ditch sometimes and Roderick's car went in all the time. Someone always came along to rescue them.

"These things happen."

"Hank, take me home,". she whispered. "I mean take me back to the funeral parlour. Or for a pizza. Or ..." And more loudly. "What a LOVELY party this has been, but Hank and I have another party, I mean ... well, we must go."

Was that polite enough?

After pizza at one restaurant and egg rolls at another and a chocolate marshmallow sundae it was morning and Hank and Roseberry started back to the funeral parlour. There was an early-morning feel about everything, as if the sun had just come up, as if the city were waking up, everything moving gradually more quickly, with purpose.

"I thought we were only gone an hour," Rose said. "Or a minute." How would Hank explain?

"I don't know," Hank said. "Time stands still. And a whole day may have passed."

He wanted then to warn her, to warn her about his paradoxes. Zeno's may have taken centuries, but if she got drawn into them maybe there was no way out. And she wanted to tell him the same thing. Stay out of my fictions. But they had ceased to belong to her as she moved on anyway. Someone else must have written them. But no matter. She would not murder again.

"I knew someone who ... she wasn't like you ... she was naive and pompous and scared and depressed. What a combination. But other than that, she was like you. Slightly crazy. Very bright. And funny. And warm. Her name ... What was her name? I forget."

It was Rosemary-berry, thought Rosemary. Rosemary-berry.

"What's in a name?" she said. "I knew someone like you once, too, and I forget his name. He was like you except for … never mind, you probably know … But, in subtraction, he WAS like you. Very bright. Very attractive. And funny. And…" She looked puzzled. She really had forgotten his name, walked on in a dazed state of almost grasping everything, but not grasping anything yet.

"Where do you work?" Hank asked as they walked down the hall of the funeral parlour and the attendant bowed towards them. Forgetting where they were. Talking to her as if they had just been introduced. Perhaps at a cocktail party. And as if suddenly around them it was quiet because everyone had gone to the bar, or to another room for a while.

"At a desk," she said. "Sometimes on the floor. Occasionally in the tub. Or in a park. It's VERY NICE to work in a park." And suddenly she really was not frightened of him. And she did not think he knew everything and she knew nothing, as she had thought the last time. Whenever that was. She might even tell him about the park where she liked to lie on the grass and watch bees in the clover and leaves rustling in the breeze. Sometime, now that she would never again tell anyone everything, she might tell Hank that. "Where do you work?" she asked.

"At a desk. At a hundred desks." He looked discouraged.

"Desks are all right," she said. "I always have to return to my desk in the end."

"Um," he said. "But it's VERY NICE to work in a park."

The discreet, polite man was standing at the other end of the hall holding a door for them. It wasn't the door with the chain. There were no bodies.

"You go out this way," he said.

"Which direction?" Rosemary asked as she stepped toward the door, puzzled.

"It depends where you're going."

"I don't know," she said.

These things happen.

Hannah's Drawings

PATRICK COULD STILL GO out for appointments, but no one knew how much longer he would have. In meeting with the hospice team, I had hoped to learn more about him. But I still knew very little when I was greeted that first afternoon by a small girl with red hair and freckles at the door of his apartment overlooking the Don Valley Parkway.

"You must be Martin," the child said.

"And you must be Hannah."

She nodded. "I'm going down the hall to my friend's place," she said. "But my Mom's here. And my Dad."

As I entered the apartment, the first thing I saw was a kaleidoscope of brilliant yellows and reds – I could make out a bicycle, wheels – in a painting hanging above the sofa. Patrick's wife, Rose, saw me admire it.

"A Curnoe," she said. She moved across the living room, her shadow on the wall almost bouncing after her as she picked up a straw purse and a large striped umbrella. "I'm glad to meet you, Martin. Thanks for coming. I wish I could stay and chat, but I'm already late for my appointment at the naturopath's." The door clicked behind her.

Patrick shook my hand, then turned on Beethoven's third symphony, *Eroica*, the one the composer himself conducted when it was first performed in Vienna. As I listened, I sat back on the sofa and looked around the room. It reminded me of my first apartments, with furniture both sparse and spartan. In contrast, many paintings hung on all the walls, mainly watercolours, from a vivid palette that brightened the room like rays of sunlight.

They're Rose's," Patrick said. "She loves to paint."

As I glanced at colourful drawings plastered in the most unlikely places – on a table leg, on the ceiling – he added, "Those
are Hannah's." He pointed overhead. "I can see that one when I'm
lying down."

But the music was too loud for sustained conversation. Indeed,
Patrick said almost nothing more until it came time for me to leave.
Then he grunted something I couldn't make out.

"I'll see you next week," I said.

It was Patrick's pattern to turn on classical music as soon as I arrived. He would name the composer. Handel, Greig, Beethoven,
Schubert. It seemed to please him that I was familiar with most of
his selections. Although a nod or a grunt might be all that conveyed
that pleasure

"I'm a bit of a musician myself," he said gruffly one day. "Although
not a professional."

He took a violin from behind his chair and started to tune it. He
frowned. "I can't play very well any more." It wasn't long before he
put the instrument away.

Week after week, I kept my regular appointments – four-hour
stretches. The music is what stands out. Even sitting in traffic, perhaps behind a streetcar on Queen Street waiting to find a parking
spot so Patrick could go for x-rays at the hospital, the radio was
always on. Usually the CBC, but occasionally the station in Cobourg
that played classical music.

When he could no longer come out with me in his car, I often
picked up little things for Patrick. I was retired by then and happy
to run various errands for him. Sometimes I just dropped by in my
small truck to say hello and see how he was doing. I would catch
myself whistling Beethoven. My wife, chuckling, would comment
that I must be thinking about Patrick. And as the days and weeks
passed, he and Rose became my friends.

There were always magazines on the coffee table. Some on ho-
meopathy, others on ways of managing pain such as acupuncture,
and books on healing by Deepak Chopra. They spent most of their
money looking for things to help Patrick feel more comfortable. And

even for something more than that. New herbal or homeopathic remedies. Something the doctors would not have thought about. Although they did find out what treatments were offered by places like the Mayo Clinic. They never said they hoped for a cure, but I could tell. Hope, the mysterious element that keeps people going. Or some kind of faith, I suppose. My wife and I have begun to go to church occasionally. Doris also works for the hospice. We don't talk about dying a lot, more the little nuances of change in the people we're visiting, the small details of what we might have done to help out that day.

As Patrick became increasingly weaker, the team moved his bed to the living room. His head was propped up and facing places in the room that Rose and five-year-old Hannah hung out. Nearby was an intravenous ready for whenever it might be needed.

"I wonder Martin, could you stay a little longer today?" Rose asked one Wednesday.

"Of course."

"Patrick and I have decided what we want when he dies."

"Would you help Rose?" Patrick asked, his voice fainter now and more difficult to hear. "When the time comes."

"Of course."

"We don't want an ordinary funeral."

"No," Rose said.

I nodded. I knew it wouldn't be long now. By then I knew Patrick's movements, the way he closed his eyes when he was deep into the sounds of a favourite piece of music. He particularly liked Bach and Mozart. Schubert, too. Before I left that day, he listened to the first refrain of the unfinished eighth symphony.

"I don't know why it was never completed," he muttered to no one in particular. "He did go on and write the ninth." He didn't add, as he had once before, that maybe it had something to do with the syphilis Schubert had contracted when working on it.

I was still listening to the music playing in my head when I drove away in my truck and even as I opened the door of our house forty-five or so minutes later. The telephone was ringing and I rushed to pick up the receiver, as if I knew it would be Rose. And it was.

"Did I leave something behind?" I asked, hopefully.

"Patrick's just died."

I took in a deep breath. "Are you all right?"

"I think so." Then, "Do you suppose you could go to the funeral parlour and pick up the coffin? I've just phoned them to say someone will come. By the time you get here, the coroner should have been already. I called the doctor."

"Where is Patrick now?"

"In the living room," Rose said. "In his bed."

I had to drink a huge glass of cold water when I hung up and then sit down. My father died when I was in my teens, in a village in Devon on the south coast of England. My mother never talked about him afterward and my older sisters and brothers had already left home by then. I didn't know there was another way to cope with the loss other than to go on as if nothing had happened. All the same, I missed my father.

We lived in a house with a thatched roof that looked out over fields where there were sheep and apple orchards. My father walked early each morning down the road to work at the post office and came back in the evenings through the fields. He was a quiet man, but friendly with all the customers and he was popular in the village. He helped organize an annual theatre night and played a minor role in one of the performances each year as well. He asked me to play Prince Charming when I was seven and encouraged my interest in theatre. I thought about him all the way to the funeral parlour to get Patrick's coffin. A cardboard box so light it was easy to carry out to the truck.

The man in the funeral parlour was dressed in a dark suit and tie. He had the sombre manner of someone you could count on. So when it started to rain as I slid the coffin into the back of the truck, I went back inside to ask him if I could have a sheet of plastic.

He looked baffled. "What for?"

"I'm driving a pickup," I explained before he relented and went to see what he could find.

I placed the clear plastic he gave me over the cardboard coffin and tucked it underneath. When I realized I didn't have any rope to tie the coffin down, so light that it might well blow off as I drove across the city, I was too embarrassed to ask for anything else. So I drove very slowly back to Rose's apartment. When I reached the high rise that looked down on the Parkway, with the traffic below sounding like a river rushing through a canyon, I parked near the front door and then buzzed Rose from the lobby. I was carrying the coffin in a perpendicular position, hoping it looked like a refrigerator carton.

Patrick's death was so different from anything I'd previously experienced. It took years before I could even talk about the death of my father. Instead, I went on canoe trips in Algonquin Park and on hikes in the Gatineau Hills. These outings soothed me. I would gaze at the stars at night, watch for the first loon at dawn, and look for animals in the woods. Sometimes I would paddle for eight or nine hours at a stretch, until I was exhausted. I would set up my green tent on a campsite, making sure my backpack was hung from a tree so bears would stay away. Only much later was I aware that I was shutting Doris out and that the pain of my father's death was still with me. When I began to do volunteer work for the hospice, we finally began to talk about it.

When I stepped into the elevator, a man and two women looked at me oddly. They didn't say anything. I watched the numbers flash as we passed the floors. When I stepped out, coffin clasped in front of me, I walked down the corridor to Rose and Patrick's apartment and tapped gently on the door. Then a little louder.

"I'm so glad you're here," Rose said as she opened the door and motioned me inside.

We hugged for a long time and then she asked me to put the coffin on the dining room table. Together we lifted Patrick from the bed and placed him inside. He had lost so much weight that he wasn't heavy at all, but it was awkward, and sad, moving his inert form from the bed to the coffin. Rose closed the cover. There were tears in her eyes, and mine.

"The coroner's been here already," she said. "Hannah's down the hall, playing with her friend. But the last couple of hours she was sitting with Patrick." Rose said she had closed his mouth so it wasn't wide and gaping, his eyes also, although they flicked opened again and stared at her. It was disconcerting.

"I'll make tea," I said.

We sat down on the brown couch across from the table and talked about going to the mausoleum the next day. And dealing with all the small details as Patrick would have wanted.

"Could we use your truck again?" she asked.

The next day when I returned to the apartment, the sun was shining on the coffin and Hannah was sitting on it. She was drawing pictures on the firm cardboard with bright coloured crayons. Her friend from down the hall was with her, also drawing. Hannah looked up once and grinned at me, then went on colouring a little house with trees around it. A dog and cat. Some people.

Visitors came and went all day. When they saw what the children were doing, they signed their names on the coffin. After a while, I picked up some crayons and drew a picture of a robin. It struck me Patrick would like the robin.

The following day, the coffin wasn't on the table.

"It's out on the balcony," Rose said. "When my sister arrived, she suggested it would be cooler out there."

We carried it back into the living room.

Rose put a light tan shawl over her shoulders, one she had crocheted while sitting with Patrick. She wore a taupe dress and a yellow flower in her hair. On her feet were her usual Birkenstocks.

"I'll find Hannah," she said. "Then we can go. They're expecting us at the mausoleum. Patrick made all the arrangements some time ago. They were ready to hear from me."

We followed the yellow line in the middle of the road that curves its way through Mount Pleasant Cemetery to a big, grey building and parked in the lot on the far side.

"I'll go and see what to do," Rose said.

She returned with two men who said they would take the coffin. We followed them around to the crematorium. Hannah was standing next to me beside the truck when Rose's sister drove up in her small white Honda.

Inside Rose took out her prayer book. She began to read, leaning slightly over the coffin, now covered with signatures and bright drawings. "The Lord is my shepherd," she read and continued on through to the end of the twenty-third psalm. When she was finished, she and Hannah read a poem together.

Do not stand at my grave and weep;
I am not there, I do not sleep.
I am a thousand winds that blow.
I am the diamond that glints on snow.
I am the sunlight of ripened grain.
I am the gentle autumn rain....

When the poem ended, I watched the men put the coffin into the retort, the chamber in the cremation furnace where the body is placed. We stood and watched flames engulf it, the two sisters holding each other, Hannah in the middle. I put my hand on Rose's shoulder. I felt her tremble and heard her stifled sobs. It wasn't until the fire burned down that she stopped.

"Could I have the ashes in two containers?" she asked.

"I'll pick them up tomorrow," I said softly.

"One's for the garden," she told me when I brought them to her the next day. "My mother's garden, the house where I grew up, where Patrick and I lived for the first two years we were together." She was talking about the family home on a hill overlooking Lake Ontario. "The other is to go into a brick for an extension mother is building."

In the original house, her father's ashes were in one of the bricks and Rose wanted to continue the tradition.

I nodded, wondering what any new buyers of that house might think if they knew, if they would wonder about ghosts. Or if anyone would even tell them.

Rose and Patrick made death an ongoing part of life. They shared that with me. And I learned that death wasn't what I thought it was. Sometimes it's painful and drawn out, but there are moments of humour. I remember one day when Patrick was impatient and wondered why, if he were dying, he was still here. So you go on being here until you're not, I guess. I don't know where you go after that. It's more than ashes in cans. Or urns. Or bodies in caskets. Something stays with us.

My father was a gentleman who didn't have a lot of ambition and that used to irritate my mother. She wanted him to make something of himself. Not go off walking in the woods, looking for flowers. Not read his books of poetry and sit in an old armchair, listening to the birds sing outside the window. I think I know why. There's something in nature that soothes you. Like music. But my mother never appreciated that. Nor was she enthusiastic about his role in the local theatre group. I wonder what she hoped for in her life. Whatever it was, my father disappointed her.

He might be surprised that I've used what I learned as a boy in the village theatre nights to become somewhat of a storyteller. Standing at the centre of a circle of volunteers from the hospice, a new team forming to support a retired teacher who has become so frail her legs are like sticks now, I recently strung out a story for fifteen or twenty minutes. When I started, I was thinking that you can still see the face of a younger woman in her luminous blue eyes, which light up when you go into the front room where she often lies on the couch with her ginger tabby cat. The couch is covered with bright cushions – red, orange, yellow, green – and her shelves are lined with books. She likes to talk, but she tires quickly. She's reading a book about global politics and the environmental movement. Something else about the care of the soul.

"You never know what you'll be asked to do at a hospice," I said.

Then I began to tell them about Patrick. When I reached the part about Hannah sitting on the coffin with her crayons, drawing bright pictures and colouring them, everyone laughed. Even a man with AIDS, thin and wan, whom I could see was having difficulty when I started the story, laughed out loud.

It's a gift that comes from those early days in the village, from going out onto the stage, from my father, that I can stand up and talk about something so serious and yet make people laugh.

When I was in England last year, I went to the country church where my father is buried. As a boy I often stood by his grave. But last year I couldn't remember where it was in the graveyard and I had to search desperately to find it. I was so upset, I cried. It was only when I turned to leave that I stumbled on the grave. I stood quietly then.

"Thank you for what you gave me, father," I said. "And farewell and Godspeed."

When a note came from Rose recently, I felt things had come full circle. She had enclosed a picture of her and Hannah taken on Salt Spring Island where they're renting a small house in a town where the ferries from the mainland arrive each day.

Hannah has started to go to school and has found a new friend who lives near by, she wrote. *She talks about Patrick often and asks a lot of questions. We scattered his ashes in the garden overlooking the water before we left and the brick will soon be in the new wall that faces Lake Ontario.*

Hannah, only six now, knows more than most of us. Although I think my father would be proud of me.

Two Women in Venice

VENICE WASN'T EVEN ON the itinerary she left on the kitchen table for Frank. But Birgit nonetheless finds herself in the railroad station there on a bright afternoon in November, listening to the sounds of another language. On the train across northern Italy, she met no one who spoke English and her few words of Italian are merely functional. But ever since Frank was invited here to give a paper to a group of scholars gathered from around the world to discuss issues in theology, Birgit has to admit, even if only to herself, that she has wanted to come. At the time, she suggested that she accompany him.

"Why don't you take a trip yourself when you start to get your old age pension?" he asked.

At the thought that she has finally plunged into this journey, her head aches. She's too old for this. As Birgit stands in line at the exchange counter, she looks around the station for a tourist information kiosk. A woman in her mid-forties comes up behind her. There's a red, white and blue flag with the stars and stripes on her backpack.

Someone who speaks English?

They soon exchange names, the American is Mary-Tom, and discover that both of them have been getting around on Eurail passes, that the American woman landed at Schipol in Amsterdam.

"And you?" she asks.

"Paris," Birgit says. She veered off in this direction impulsively, after all that's why she bought a train pass. She can go somewhere just because she feels like it. So a few months after her sixty-fifth birthday, here she is.

"I stayed for a few nights on the Left Bank."

"Where will you stay here?" Mary-Tom asks.

"I don't know yet."

Frank stayed in an expensive hotel on the Grand Canal, near San Marco, arranged by a travel agent months before he flew to Milan and caught the train to Venice. She doesn't think he would risk arriving somewhere any more and taking whatever he found.

"There's a pension which looks out at the Giudecca Canal," Mary-Tom says. "It's quite wonderful. Would you consider sharing a room?"

As they lug their bags to the pension from a *vaporetta*, one of the large water taxis on the Grand Canal, Mary-Tom stops to study the lines of the gondolas in a repair yard.

"The shapes are different depending on whether they're built for one or two gondoliers." She takes out a small blue notebook and begins to jot down a few words. "For a story." She also does a quick sketch on one of the blank pages.

When they reach the room, Mary-Tom goes to the window and looks out at the sky. "We're really here," she sighs. "This is Venice. Isn't it wonderful?"

"You didn't tell me how you got your name," Birgit says. "Where did it come from?"

Mary-Tom smiles. "My father's name is Tom," she says. "He liked it and decided to use it for his first child whether it was a boy or a girl. And the first child was me. My family's like that."

"Why are you travelling alone?" Birgit asks.

Mary-Tom shrugs. "The usual," she says. "None of my friends were free." She looks at a snapshot of two boys in their late teens or early twenties she has put on the night table. "They're at college," she says. "What about you?"

"My husband was busy," Birgit says. "We don't do much together any more." She twists the ring on her left hand. "Sometimes we walk the dog." Quite unexpectedly, Frank will ask if she wants to accompany him and the black Labrador retriever, Marco Polo.

As Mary-Tom starts to write again, Birgit thinks of the blank pages of the notebook that she bought in the airport in Toronto. She has so much stored away she could tell. While the children were growing up, she was forever packing the family's belongings into trunks and boxes to follow her husband to some unlikely location. Their youngest daughter was born in China where Frank was a missionary until Mao Tse Tung took over.

"There," Mary-Tom says. "That's done." She looks up at the notebook Birgit is now fingering tentatively. "Do you write, too?"

There are advantages to being old. She has seen whole societies that no longer exist. Works of art that were destroyed by war in Europe still live in her memory. Maybe she will travel up through the Brenner Pass to the spot in the Alps outside Innsbruck where her grandparents lived and to the small town on the Rhine she hasn't visited since her family left Germany to emigrate to Canada when she was a teenager.

"Why don't you?" Mary-Tom asks.

Birgit feels exposed at the thought of her handwriting on one of the blank pages, almost as if she's been caught undressing in front of a window. She undoes the braid that circles her head and lets her hair hang loose down her back. She turns to look at the moon rising over the Lido. When Frank asked her for a divorce twenty years earlier, she was frightened and said she'd rather not do anything. Even though she knew things weren't going well and had said more than once that she wanted to leave.

"Then let's not talk about it ever again," Frank said.

He built a studio over the garage where he often sat late at night, listening to music or playing the piano, and gradually they took separate bedrooms.

Birgit picks up her toothbrush and goes over to the sink. When she crawls under the sheet, she tosses and turns for a long time. She listens to the even breathing from the bed across from her. When Mary-Tom gulps and snores in one loud roar, Birgit wishes she could prod her as she prodded Frank when they still slept together. Finally he would roll onto his stomach with a huge sigh, but she can't do that to a stranger. As the snoring continues, she leaps from her bed and grabs a book. There's a toilet in a small bathroom connected to the bedroom with a window that also looks out on the night sky and she'll sit there and read until she's so sleepy nothing can bother her.

As Birgit flips through the pages, she has an image of walking with Frank and Marco Polo through the ravine down behind the Rosedale subway station. Of leaves turning red and golden and the big black dog running after a stick. When she finally crawls back under the blankets, the springs creak and she glances across at the still form in the other bed, worried the noise may have woken her. Mary-Tom rolls sleepily toward the night table between them and switches on the lamp. She looks at her watch and turns the light off again. Birgit considers telling her she's been snoring, but soon she hears even breathing again. She wonders what she'll do in the morning and if Mary-Tom will want to go off on her own. She supposes she could walk around San Marco and peer up at the splendid Byzantine architecture of the Basilica. Finally she falls asleep and dreams there's a tiny baby in a pod in a corner of her backpack. She's amazed anything so small can be so perfect. There are two other babies someone throws from a train. She catches the smaller one, but then she has no arms. The next is thrown gently and lands on the ground beside her. She tries to pick it up, but she can't hold any of the babies. She wakes up gasping for breath.

"HELP!" she calls.

When Birgit rolls over, the bed beside her is empty. She dresses in the bathroom where Mary-Tom's white towel hangs on the open window. Then she goes down the five flights of stairs to the small dining room, the tables covered with red tablecloths, the owner pointed out in halting English the previous night. When she walks in, she sees Mary-Tom sitting near the window. She thinks of how Frank looks blankly at her when he comes into the kitchen in the morning. She waited for him to complete graduate school. She waited in China until they could leave after the Communists took over. For the girls to grow up. For her grandchildrens' births. What is she waiting for now?

"Did you get some sleep?" Mary-Tom asks.

"Yes, thanks," Birgit says.

Steam rises from the spout of the pot as she pours coffee into her cup. She told one of her grandchildren, the smallest girl, Jenny, that there was a fairy in their Limoges teapot in Toronto.

"How does it get out?" Jenny asked.

Birgit breaks a roll and looks up to find Mary-Tom watching her. "We get better Italian bread than this in Toronto," she says. "You must in New York, too." She visualizes the apartment the American woman has described, overlooking the Hudson River.

"Which direction did we go last night?" the younger woman asks as Birgit spreads a map out beside her placemat.

Birgit traces her finger along the circuitous route that must have been the one that led them away from rather than towards San Marco.

"Have you decided where to go today?" Mary-Tom's voice trails off and she looks away, one hand tapping the table.

Birgit watches her companion with a puzzled frown as she runs her finger over the map again, along the Grand Canal towards San Marco. "Here," she says, visualizing the square with the golden spires of the Basilica at one end of it.

"May I come with you?"

"Oh yes," Birgit says eagerly. A sense of relief surges through her as she wonders if under the confident exterior Mary-Tom also minds travelling unaccompanied.

"It will help me write about Venice if I can see it through your eyes, too," Mary-Tom says.

"Um," Birgit murmurs.

When they emerge from the Basilica two hours later, Mary-Tom smiles brightly.

"I noticed a cosy *trattoria*," Birgit says, gesturing towards the square. She wonders what she would do if even now Frank decided to leave her. How would she manage?

"Let's see the Doge's palace first," Mary-Tom says. "And then after lunch we can go to the Rialto."

Birgit agrees and once inside the palace, she begins to point out paintings she recognizes to Mary-Tom.

"Can you recognize a Tintoretto?" Birgit asks.

"Not yet," Mary-Tom says. "But with your help, it sounds as if I'll soon be able to."

Birgit nods, aware that they could be mistaken for mother and daughter. She's pleased at the thought she'll be able to talk about art to someone who is receptive. Share what she knows. It happens so seldom these days. "We'll have to go to the Accademia, too. There are paintings there from every period of Italian history."

"Where are you going after Venice?" Mary-Tom asks.

"I don't know yet," Birgit says. She remembers that as a young child when she went shopping with her grandmother in the village in Austria, she imagined she lived there. Maybe it was important to go back now.

"Geneva. Lucerne. Zurich," Frank said as he studied her itinerary. "What about Innsbruck?"

"No," she said abruptly.

"And Germany?"

"NO."

Frank lit his pipe then with a quizzical expression on his face. "Why?" he asked. Although he knew why. It's such a long time since she's thought of her father's loud voice wafting up the valley as he walked along the Rhine toward their house at the end of the village. He had sung so loudly on his way home that everyone knew Christof Maul had had too much to drink again. And Birgit would cringe in her bed, anticipating the arguments that would follow his return. What good would it do to go back there now?

"How do I get from the Rialto to the pension?" Mary-Tom murmurs.

Birgit shows her what streets and canals to follow.

Mary-Tom looks up then. "I'm sorry," she says. "Do you mind if I go alone? It's my first trip since my divorce and I just need to wander."

"I'll see you later."

Birgit is surprised at the sudden change in plans, but she almost understands. And walks slowly in a different direction, observing the narrow passageway she approaches and a boat laden with vegetables that stops at the back door of a building. A man in another boat waves at the first and shouts a greeting. Birgit reaches in her bag for her notebook. Maybe she'll begin to make notes after all. Would she start with the town nestled on the banks of the Rhine? Later she could contemplate China. It flashes before her in kaleidoscopic fashion, almost as if she were finally coming full circle. Somehow she has to prepare for whatever awaits her. Even after forty years with Frank, she really doesn't know what she'll find when she returns. But the page remains blank and she walks on instead. At a small bakery she buys some bread that appears more authentic than what she'd had for breakfast and some fruit and cheese at another store.

"*Uno etto*," she says haltingly as the man behind the counter takes out the cheese she points out.

"Asiago," he says.

"*Grazie.*"

In a courtyard near a pension, she hears the loud shrieks of children and peers in to see a soccer game in progress. A rotund priest blows the whistle at the end of a play. She moves on slowly. At the edge of the canal, Birgit sits on a bench and watches the boats and gondolas ply their way back and forth on the water. When she returns to Toronto, she will mention divorce. Yes, after all these years, she will mention it.

After a while, she dozes and dreams she's on a plane over Africa. The plane flies so low that the ground is close enough to see rocks in a stream and mountains and hills above. They land smoothly in rough terrain, yet it isn't a helicopter. Birgit is shocked to find she can see all this, then realizes it's because the nose of the plane is a window and there's no pilot to obstruct the view. The people all get off in the dark. At that moment, Birgit realizes she hasn't had any of the shots she should have had for the trip. She doesn't know where they are, or why, or what she's doing there.

When she awakens she can feel that her face has reddened slightly in the sun. She's glad when she hears Mary-Tom's voice call out a greeting. Scarcely able to believe it was just the previous day they met, she looks up and waves. But she'll have to leave soon. At the station, she had noted a train that leaves for Munich each day at noon. There are also trains to Rome and Florence and many other destinations, but it's the one to Munich that makes connections to routes spanning out all over Germany that draws her now. However, it isn't until they are seated at dinner that she tells her companion that within the next day or so she'll be leaving Venice.

Mary-Tom smiles, but she looks a little sad. "I'll miss you," she says.

"Yes," Birgit says. "Meeting you felt as if it were meant to happen."

"Thank you," Mary-Tom says. Then her demeanour changes and her voice softens. "I'll have to take a smaller room when the time comes," she muses. "But that's all right. I could ask for one with a desk, I suppose." Her eyes glaze over. "But I'm not quite sure where to begin."

"You could describe the woman you're sharing with, the woman with the old age pension and the backpack."

"I could," Mary-Tom says. "But that's your story."

"How would you write it?"

"About walking the dog. About travelling alone for the first time. About going back to explore roots, then going back to Canada and —"

"Getting a divorce," Birgit says. Isn't that the obvious outcome that has been there on the horizon for as long as she can recall?

"Well, that's one possibility. But there are others."

"You think so? Maybe he's found a young lover. That's what men do, isn't it? Find young lovers who put them on pedestals, who keep them from facing their mortality."

"I don't know. Do they?" Mary-Tom asks.

"And women," Birgit says. "What do we do?"

"Some have affairs with older married men," Mary-Tom says. She apologizes when she sees Birgit's face.

"Don't apologize," Birgit says. "Some of them undoubtedly do."

There could be a younger woman even now. It wouldn't be the

first one.

"Actually another ending could be renewed interest. Just think of all you'll have to tell after a trip like the one you're embarked on."

Birgit chuckled. "Oh well, imagination is a wonderful thing, isn't it? I never thought of that."

"Would you like to exchange addresses?" Mary-Tom asks. "You can send me the story."

"What story?" Birgit asks, feeling herself pushed in a direction she doesn't understand yet. Even though that notebook is in her purse, and she carries it everywhere on this trip. As if it has a purpose.

"*Two Women In Venice,* perhaps. Or, *The Woman With the Old Age Pension and the Backpack.*"

"*A few months after my sixty-fifth birthday, I find myself en route to Venice,*" Birgit says. "*On the train across northern Italy, I meet no one who speaks English and my few words of Italian are merely functional.*"

"Get out your notebook," Mary-Tom says. "Get it down. Even before you return home, fill pages and pages and pages. Get it down."

For a moment they are both silent. "*It was the trip of a lifetime,*" Mary-Tom intones. "*One she had meant to take with her husband. Instead here she was alone in Amsterdam while he climbed Mount Kilimanjaro with someone he had met on an airplane.*"

"Is that what happened?"

"No, I made it up." A frown crosses the younger woman's face. "But there's some resemblance to the truth. It's not Mount Kilimanjaro and he met her at the office. But whatever the truth and the fiction, he's out there with new twat."

The two women look at each other and burst into gales of laughter.

When their gaiety subsides, Birgit reaches into her purse and fingers the binding of her notebook. She can visualize the sentence she uttered spontaneoulsy just moments earlier starting to flow over the first page. It doesn't matter where the story leads her, she wants to tell it.

Hats

"THIS WOMAN WITH THE backpack doesn't have any idea what she's doing," the man behind the counter at Charles de Gaulle Airport said to his colleague behind the next wicket. "All she has to do is read the signs."

"*Excusez-moi*," Libby said, standing taller and staring into his steely eyes as he sneered down his long, narrow nose at her. Even before she struggled for words to ask where to catch the train into Paris, he had the gall to insult her. "I might have difficulty saying what I'm looking for, but I can understand you." She pursed her lips and brushed a stray stand of greying hair from her forehead. It sure wasn't like growing up in Quebec where she was able to throw in a few words in English and still make herself understood.

Her children had encouraged her to take this trip. They gave her tapes of Francis Cabrel's songs and on her fiftieth birthday put a fleur-de-lys over the front door of the house in downtown Toronto. Paul, who had spent over a month sleeping on Greek beaches, came and helped her decide what to pack. She didn't need half of what she thought she did, he said. Rosemary said she would water the plants and pick up all the flyers left between the rails of the porch. They assured her they would visit their grandmother. Her mother hadn't wanted her to come. From the time Libby mentioned it, it was apparent she was uneasy.

The man jerked his head to look at her. "*Pardon, Madame*," he said. He came out from behind the counter. With a flourish, he asked if Madame had a reservation somewhere.

" *Oui.*" A small hotel on the Left Bank she heard about from a woman sitting next to her when she had her hair cut at a salon in Toronto.

"It's not cheap, but it's not expensive either," the woman told her.

"And the concièrge! He's wonderful."

"*Ah oui, Madame,*" the man said. "*Ici. Changez ici à Gare du Nord et —*"

So she was soon on a train travelling past brown houses with clay tile roofs, on her way to a Metro stop on the Left Bank where she would emerge and follow a route marked now in black pen on her map. What struck her as she looked out the window was how many stories the endless doors in the houses must hide.

When she arrived in the lobby, a short, round man with red cheeks and a blue denim apron greeted her. "*Votre chambre est prête,*" he said, a smile brightening his dour countenance. He saw visitors all the time who had just come in on overnight flights across the Atlantic. "*Vous serez mieux après avoir dormi pour quelques heures.*" He walked slowly across the lobby to the elevator with her. She'd like the room, he said. He kept one with a window that looked out over the street, up high enough so it would be quiet. He pointed to blue and white checked tablecloths as they passed the dining area. Breakfast was served there.

"*Entre sept et neuf heures,*" he said. "*Croissants. Chocolat chaud.*" She'd like that also.

The elevator moved slowly up to the third floor where he opened a door with a large key. She looked dubiously at the bed that sloped toward the middle, a pale pink and blue duvet folded back on it.

"It's very comfortable," he said.

As soon as he left, she lay down on the bed to test the mattress. A little soft, but it would do. She unpacked her bag, then sat at a small table near the window, sketchbook in front of her. She'd been to Paris twice before, both quick trips. In and out in a couple of days. Once as a teenager with her parents and her younger brother, imagine all that way from a small mining town in northern Quebec. There were all the graves they had to see in England first, Dad's ancestors, the name Walter Muir stretching back through the generations, and where Dad was during the Second World War. It was a little village, no soldiers, none of the things Mum had read to them about from the letters he'd written. Then, whoosh, across the channel in an airplane for two nights in Paris. Maybe because Libby said she wanted to go to France and she was the oldest or maybe because Mum had a grandmother who hadn't spoken English. But for whatever reasons, they went. Then Dad left Mum and the kids to cross the ocean on a Cunard liner while he flew back to the mine ahead of them. Drunk on the station platform when they arrived a couple of weeks later. All the time they were in England, he wasn't. Even with all the wine in France, he managed. Well, she didn't have to worry about him any more; he'd been dead for ten years. She didn't have to worry about Barton either. She was with him on the second trip when they did the typical sightseeing thing – Eiffel Tower, Notre Dame, Montmartre. Barton had a good time, but he quibbled about money when they were separating, said she liked to travel too much. As if she could have squeezed that out of what he gave her for Rosemary and Paul. Well, the kids had left home and he wasn't paying her anything any more. It was a long time since she'd considered what he might think.

This time she was alone in France. It might be scary trying to figure it all out, different money, a language that was coming back to her although she was sure rusty, but she'd begun a journey she'd realized she would one day have to take. Instead of it happening years earlier, there was the long white dress and veil, the small wooden church next to the bush in northern Quebec, the reception in the house where all the furniture was moved to the basement. She had a vague sense at the time that what she was giving up was her freedom. But living somewhere across an ocean, on another continent, for any length of time seemed like a dream then rather than a real possibility. So for fifteen years, immersed in the children and increasingly bewildered and angry by Barton's efforts to thwart and change her, she'd kept some part of herself on hold.

Out on the street, she gazed up at an intricate black wrought iron balcony on an old building at the corner and down into the window of a small pastry shop. *Ah, c'est merveilleux.* She would discover little cafés and bistros. She would walk along the Seine and see the stalls there; she would hear French spoken everywhere.

Exhausted and bleary-eyed, scarcely able to walk in a straight line, she remembered reading in her guidebook that there were telephones in the post office on rue de Louvre. Perhaps she would call Clare and Marcel, friends who were in Provence on sabbatical for a year. She anticipated Clare's first question.

"When are you coming?" And her next comment, "You know you're always welcome." Although she had no idea when she would visit them, it was comforting to know she had friends on this side of the ocean.

When she did find the telephones, Marcel was the one who said it. "There's always a bed for you." And she felt Clare nodding.

"Whatever else you do, see the Monet water lilies," Clare said when she took the receiver. Then added, "There's been a storm around Avignon today with fierce winds and torrential rains."

"The sun's been shining in Paris." Libby smiled at the glorious weather.

"*Trouvez quelque chose ordinaire* to watch on an ongoing basis," Marcel said.

She could visualize him beside Clare, also talking into the receiver.

"Like what?" Something ordinary to watch? Maybe she would look for pastries, croissants.

"Oh, I don't know," Clare said. She paused. "Marcel says maybe hats."

"Hats?" She was baffled.

When she went out again, the sky had clouded over and she could feel the sprinkle of a few raindrops on her face. On the other side of the Seine, chess players hovered over their boards near a bed of red flowers in the Jardin du Luxembourg, undeterred by the rain. They moved the large wooden pieces – a knight, a pawn, a bishop – and one young man pouted as he lost a game. He wore a dark navy beret that he pushed to the back of his head. Surely Marcel didn't think she'd come all this way to watch hats, but she was particularly aware of the beret in a way she likely would not have been if he hadn't mentioned them.

When she arrived back at the hotel, she caught a glimpse of the television in the lobby showing devastated areas where farmers had lost everything. The storm Clare had spoken about had also hit Normandy. She was too tired to stop and when she went up to her room and lay down, she fell asleep as soon as her head touched the pillow.

She was on a boat on the Seine and saw Barton strolling along the grassy bank with a woman. When he saw her, he shouted that he was enjoying this marriage. Then Mum's voice said she was sorry she'd had a stroke and kept her from taking her trip.

"But you didn't. Can't you see I'm already in Paris?"

When she woke up, it was a moment before she could figure out where she was. And by the time she changed into something comfortable, it was time for breakfast. When she finally got downstairs, she was surprised to find the tables were already almost full.

"Do you mind?" she asked a man who was alone.

Barton always hated the way she talked so easily with strangers. Long after they separated, she used to find herself explaining to some imaginary presence that when you grew up in a town like Bourlamaque you talked to everyone. It took a long time for her to recognize her conversations didn't warrant his suspicions.

"*Pas de tout,*" the man said. Not at all.

He sipped a cup of coffee as she drank hot chocolate. He was on vacation from the Ivory Coast where his wife worked for the Austrian embassy. He'd worked for the French foreign service, but it created problems for the marriage. Now he was in private business.

"*Et vous?*"

"On vacation from Canada," she said in French, the words gradually coming more easily.

"People who know more than one language from earliest childhood lack a sense of roots," he said. "I know two now. French and German. But my wife learned both as a child."

"Most people spoke at least two languages where I grew up."

"*Et les racines?* Do you have a sense of them?" Did she have a sense of her roots? Not really. Maybe that's what she was here discover.

Two men in dark suits and ties stopped at the table and greeted him. Pushing back his chair, he wiped his mouth with his napkin. Libby didn't even have a chance to fumble with her answer, but she knew he'd hit a sore spot. She was always more comfortable when she heard French around her. But like the graves in England with Muir written on them, that was only part of it.

"*Alors. C'était un plaisir, Madame.*"

As he walked to a table where the other men were already pulling out chairs, she pondered how strangers can sometimes ask just the right question to help you clarify your thoughts. When she finished her breakfast, he waved as she left the dining room.

At the market on rue Mouffetard, Libby bought a pear, a banana, and a bright red apple for her lunch. She noticed small things. Children in a nearby park, dressed like diminutive adults. From there, she went to the Picasso Museum, later walked along the Seine past the book and postcard vendors on the Left Bank.

And so she soaked up Paris for almost two weeks, Monet's water lilies, Rodin statues, sidewalk cafes, Notre Dame. One day when it started to rain, she took a trip on a *baton mouche* on the Seine. A young woman who wore a red plaid tam sat with a man in a shiphand's blue and grey striped toque, deep in conversation. As she watched them, Libby realized whether she'd come all this way to see hats or not, she'd begun to notice them as soon as Marcel suggested it. Something to tell him when she arrived in Provence, which happened almost as soon as she stepped down from the southbound train to find both Clare and Marcel waiting on the platform in Avignon.

"Hats," she said. "I have a sketchbook full of them."

Marcel beamed. Clare looked amused.

"How's Madeleine?" Libby asked. It was on one of Clare and Marcel's earlier sabbaticals, in Devon, that she and their youngest daughter became friends.

"I worry about her," Clare said. "She's having a hard time. She comes every couple of weeks for the weekend. Although she may stop now that Richard's here." Clare shook her head in apparent disgust, but didn't add anything that would explain her reaction.

"Oh, yes," Marcel concurred with a voice that conveyed some of the same impatience. "He arrived two days ago."

"Richard?" Libby asked.

"My brother's son," Clare explained. "He goes from relative to relative. I must have told you about him. No one ever says no."

"I tried to this time," Marcel shrugged. "Not that it made any difference. He was oblivious."

"Says he's recovering from a bout of something. Like mono. Except it wasn't mono," Clare said. "But whatever it was, it's not contagious."

"Let's visit the bridge," Marcel said. "You know, the song, "*Sur le pont d'Avignon.*"

Once on the road, Clare declared, "You take your life in your hands every time you get behind the wheel in France." She seemed relieved when they arrived at an unpaved road through a valley. There were clusters of stone houses with small cemeteries surrounded by high walls. The colours of the trees and vines – reds, greens, yellows – were softened to luminous shades only seen in more northern climes in paintings. The scent of rosemary, thyme, basil, and lavender wafted around them.

"The rocks piled on the roofs are to keep the clay tiles from blowing away," Marcel said. "When the Mistral comes, it's fierce."

He parked beside a cliff near a stone house, grape vines interwoven through the lattice. There was a young man sitting on the patio wearing a straw hat with a paisley band around it tipped forward on his head.

"Do you know what I'm afraid of," Marcel muttered. "I'm afraid Richard might never leave."

"He always does," Clare said. "Just when you're getting used to him. You know that, Marcel."

On the patio, Clare introduced Libby to Richard.

"How's France?" he asked.

She didn't know how to answer the question so she let it pass by her, merely nodded.

Marcel and Clare carried bags from the trunk of the car, one overflowing with vegetables. Richard lay down on the divan and pulled the brim of his hat over his face. Libby went to the car to carry her navy backpack to the house. When the wind began to blow, she looked up to check the rocks on the roof.

"Do you suppose that's the Mistral?"

When there was no answer from Richard, she went into the kitchen, closing the door behind her. Clare and Marcel were putting lettuce and carrots in the refrigerator. Libby noticed a week old copy of *Le Monde* on the counter. She hadn't read a newspaper since leaving Canada, except a headline in Paris about the crash of the stock market. Long enough after the event that what was being labelled "Black Monday" had scarcely any meaning for her. As she flipped the pages, she saw an article about René Lévèsque and visualized him brandishing his ubiquitous cigarette. She was shocked to read he'd died. She remembered when Dad stopped saying England ruled the waves and his marching songs became relics.

Richard came in. "The wind blew my hat away," he said.

Marcel studied him coldly. "When it starts to blow, hold onto everything and run for cover." He headed upstairs.

Richard also disappeared.

"Marcel thinks Richard should find a job," Clare said and it appeared that she agreed with him.

When Libby went up to her room, at the far end of the house over the garage, she could feel the cool night air creeping in around the window that overlooked fields below. The bed was against one wall and there was a small wood table at the foot of it. The heat from the fireplace downstairs reached only as far as the next room. She shivered and crawled under the blankets. When she finally slept, she was awakened around five in the morning by roosters crowing. And after that, dogs barking. Not until she heard sounds inside the house as well though did she go down to the kitchen.

"Do you want to come into the village to buy bread?" Clare asked.

In Malaucène, they parked in front of one of the four bakeries. The baker greeted them and handed Clare two loaves still warm from the oven. Then they crossed to the other side of the street to a small shop, past old men playing *boules*, to pick up a copy of *Le Monde* for Marcel. Clare pointed out a huge church built into a wall where the pope had his summer residence when the papacy was in Avignon during the fourteenth century.

"Did you see the signs for Le Pen on the road?" Richard asked when they returned.

"Who's he?" Libby asked.

"A right wing fanatic."

"France isn't Uganda," Marcel said.

Everyone was quiet. Clare and Marcel had been living in Uganda for ten years or so when Idi Amin came to power. They left Kampala then. The signs for Le Pen made them uneasy.

"Would you like to see my study, Libby?" Marcel asked.

She remembered that he was writing the first chapter of a book ten years earlier in Devon. He rewrote the first sentence throughout her whole visit and when she left, he stood at the station with her quoting the latest version. Now he took her to the hen house where he'd set up a small desk at a window that looked out over the vineyards. From this vantage point, you could see the church in another hamlet and anyone approaching on the road below. He picked up a picture of a painting.

"To use as an illustration in the book I'm working on now," he said.

Libby recognized Rembrandt's "Night Watch."

"If I get the first sentence as I want it when you're in France, I'll be happy," he said. "You bring me luck. Do you remember Devon?"

Yes, she remembered Devon. Madeleine on the pebbled beach. Marcel's sentence. She and Clare traversing the countryside, recounting their stories to each other. They ate picnics at the sides of country roads. And visited Bath. Budleigh Salterton. A town in Cornwall. Southampton. All within range of the village in Devon. She wasn't looking for hats there, but a country graveyard where her father's ancestors were buried. There were no family graves in France that she knew of, but in Malaucène the next day she noted three hats on people around them. A typical French policeman's hat, a woman's bright red and blue kerchief and a nondescript, grey wool item on one old man. There were a number of old men milling around, but the ground was too wet for *boules*.

When they arrived at the house, Libby went upstairs and sat at the small desk in her room. A bee buzzed on the outside of the screen. She took postcards she'd bought from a paper bag. *This is the village closest to the hamlet where I'm staying*, she wrote. *And the surrounding countryside. This is the view I see from my bedroom window. Imagine.*

As she addressed the first card, Clare called up that she was ready to do a little sightseeing. Libby heard her talking to Marcel on the patio.

"Will you buy me a toothbrush," Marcel said. "Something different for a change. Red, perhaps." He chuckled. "Spare no expense."

When Libby went downstairs, the quiet was shattered by the sound of a pistol.

Clare shuddered. "The son-in-law of the neighbour," she said. "He comes from Marseilles with his wife and baby and spends his time shooting at targets."

On the way to Vaison la Romaine, they stopped at a tiny, pink shrine with a plaque inside that said it was restored in the mid-eighties. There was also an edict dated a couple of centuries earlier that said only certified indigents could steal grapes. And only between dawn and dusk. When they reached Vaison, they walked through the old part of town and stopped at a small café for cappuccino.

"How's France?" Richard asked when they returned.

Libby told him about the certified indigents, but he didn't seem particularly interested.

"On November 11th, the villagers march to the tomb that commemorates all the local men who died in the first and second world wars," Marcel said. "Anyone want to come into Malaucène with me then?"

"My father was overseas during the second world war," Libby said.

"No, thanks," Richard said.

When Libby went up to her room, there was a knock at the door. Clare poked her head in. "That Richard!" she said. "He can be so tiresome." Then she read a poem from the pad she was holding, about the olive tree behind the house, how it bent when the Mistral blew.

When she left, Libby picked up a pencil and drew a dark kerchief she'd seen on a woman in Vaison. A straw hat covered with bright flowers. The beret in le Jardin de Luxembourg, the hats on the couple on the Seine, others seen in front of the bakery. Even Richard's straw one. That night when she drifted off to sleep, everyone in her dream was wearing a hat. Barton played a piano in a house in downtown Toronto in a surgeon's green cap. Dad arrived wearing the khaki peaked one he wore in the army. He was drunk and staggered around the room looking for a bottle. The children, Rosemary and Paul, were in the backyard in tiny sun-bonnets. Only Mum, wringing her hands, *what am I to do?*, on the verandah, wasn't wearing one.

"You can either sober up or get the hell out of here," Libby said to Dad. She had said that only once in the endless years of nightmares when he staggered into one house or another. That time she awakened before he responded. Now the wonder was that he didn't do what she feared, he didn't swing out at her, no, he turned around and left. Maybe it was the French policeman's hat she was wearing. When she woke up, she hoped that some day she'd dream he came home sober.

Later on, Libby and Marcel joined the procession of villagers heading toward the graveyard. When they reached the tomb, the mayor gave a speech and children put flowers at the foot of the large head stone with names inscribed on it under the dates for both the world wars. She added a tiny Canadian flag.

For you, Dad.

When she turned around, most of the people were already walking back toward the village. Marcel was with them. She followed the stragglers to the weekly market on the main street. The stalls were all still open. There was a sign near some meat that said it was horse and at another stall was a pile of dead rabbits. She turned toward racks of clothing and bought a bright fuschia scarf, then waved at Marcel and set off to walk toward the hamlet. On the road, she met two men with guns.

"*Nous cherchons les oiseaux,*" they said. Their dogs sniffed through the long grass nearby, eager to pounce on the first bird they came upon.

When Libby arrived at the house, Clare told her Madeleine had phoned to invite her to Toulouse and to walk in the Pyrenees. She'd go to Nice first, Libby told Clare. If she caught a train out along the Riviera, she could climb the trail where Nietschze had the idea for *Zarathustra.* So it was that a couple days later, Clare and Marcel dropped her off at the station in Avignon where she boarded the southbound train for Arles, and then on to Nice, with cliffs rising up from the Mediterranean and huge pebbles on the beaches. Only to discover that what the guidebook didn't tell her was that Nietschze's trail was a steep, winding one and that half way up, she'd be exhausted. Under hot sun, following a path up toward a hill town high above the aqua shimmer of the sea, she wondered what kind of stubborn foolhardiness had lead her to take this trip. Climbing over a tree trunk that almost blocked the path, the break in it fresh from a recent storm, her face red, panting, she knew she could not return by this route.

After catching her breath at the top, Libby fell into step behind a man and two women, along a cobbled street toward a garden of cacti overlooking the sea. One of the women, sensing her presence, turned around.

"I heard you say you're driving into Nice."

They looked baffled as they nodded. Nonetheless it wasn't long before all of them were talking and they offered her a lift back down into the city. They dropped her off at a corner on a main street near her hotel where already she knew the concièrge's eldest daughter was a pharmacist in Paris and the youngest helped to run the hotel. In a city where she'd now seen the Chagall Gallery, walked on the beach, and visited the market. When she found a telephone, Libby called Madeleine.

The next afternoon, she arrived in Toulouse to find her young friend standing on the platform in a yellow slicker, raindrops glistening on her dark hair. They walked through streets of red brick buildings with delicate iron balconies, past the stained glass windows of a Jacobin monastery.

"What about Richard?" Madeleine asked. "Has he left?" Her tone was as irritated as Marcel's.

"Not that I know of. But I've been gone a few days now."

"*Ennui*, they call it," Madeleine said. "He's always been like that."

When they arrived at the apartment, it was filled with the smell of smoke.

"My roommate," Madeleine said. "She's staying overnight with her boyfriend. She never stops smoking."

In spite of the odour and the noise of cars careening past three floors below, Libby fell asleep and didn't wake up until morning. The steam from a cup of coffee rose to envelop her as Madeleine called a *gîte* to see if there was space for the night. After they packed a few clothes, Madeleine put a loaf of bread and some cheese in a backpack.

"It may be cold in the mountains," she said, her face now relaxed, her voice happy.

The train stopped for just long enough at a small village, Les Merens, for them to swing down off the steps onto the platform. Madeleine started whistling. And as soon as they settled their backpacks in a spacious room with bunks in it, they walked until large clouds descended and cloaked the green-golden peaks around them.

When they returned to the *gîte*, two men and a woman had also arrived from Toulouse. One of the men said he worked as a tour guide in Carcassonne. They'd find going there interesting, he said. So much history. He fished in his pocket and took out a small pin with a red maple leaf on a white background.

"A tourist gave it to me," he said proudly. "It's the Quebec flag."

Libby and Madeleine, sprawled out on a couch in front of the fireplace, glanced surreptitiously at each other.

"It's the Canadian flag," Libby said finally.

"That's right," the man said. He moved toward the long wooden table just behind the couch where a young woman was ladling garlic soup into bowls. He opened a bottle of wine. "Will you join us?" he asked.

"What did people in Canada think about de Gaulle's *'Québec libre'* comment a few years ago?" the woman asked. "And what will happen now that Lévèsque's dead?"

Libby couldn't answer either question, but although it all felt very far away at that moment, they had a lively, spirited conversation. When she and Madeleine finally stretched out later after leaving the others to climb up to a loft in the main building, she was exhausted. Madeleine pulled her socks over her navy sweat pants before she crawled into her bed across from Libby's at a right angle. Pipes rattled and heat finally began to seep into the room.

"Sometimes I think I have the *ennui* gene. Like Richard," Madeleine said.

"Hardly."

"All the same," Madeleine said, "I'm fed up with almost everything."

"Why not go to Malaucène for a visit? You can ignore Richard."

Soon after, Libby drifted off to dream she was riding north on the subway in Toronto, past the cemetery where leaves on the trees were turning bright crimson and yellow. Where Dad's ashes were entombed and where there was a niche for Mum. Suddenly she saw Marcel.

"*Bonjour,*" he said. "I'm sorry about your divorce."

"Barton has a nice wife now."

"He already had a nice wife."

When she woke up, Madeleine was still sleeping. Back at the apartment in Toulouse, Libby would lie down on the narrow cot and close the door to keep the smell of smoke out. She could see why Madeleine preferred the Pyrenees. All the same, she wasn't unhappy when the time came to head back. And after visiting the cathedral, an art gallery, the monastery, Libby decided to go back to Malaucène.

"There's a bus from Avignon," Madeleine told her as she carried Libby's pack to the station platform. She said she would call Clare to let her know Libby would be on it.

So Libby wasn't surprised when, a few hours later, she stepped down onto the main street in the village and saw Clare coming out of the pharmacy.

"How's France?" her friend called.

France was people she'd met now, Libby thought, and the shapes of buildings, the deep greens in the Pyrenees and red bricks of Toulouse, the shimmer of the Mediterranean, marketplaces. The scent of lavender. Vineyards. Local wines. The *gîte* in Les Merens. The Left Bank. The Monet water lilies. The chess players in the Jardin de Luxembourg. She'd arrived at a cathedral in Toulouse at noon and they said they were closing for two hours while everyone had lunch. Not like North America where the main focus was what you did for a living. It was food and wine here. Food and wine and taking time to eat and drink. *Bon appetit!* Yes, fresh bread every morning. Clare and Marcel's kitchen. The village. The sound of French around her. She could feel her own memories emerging. Something about growing up in a small town in the northern Quebec bush where there were many languages. But mainly French and English. Libby felt more rooted in both of them now. It struck her that she might not have known what she was doing, but she'd still found what she was looking for. And the fragments that hadn't quite cohered had fallen into place on this trip her children had somehow also known she had to take.

A man wearing a hat with narrow purple, red and blue stripes came out of the bakery. It was pulled down over his forehead. He carried a small sack.

Libby laughed. "*Regardez le chapeau*," she said, already hearing herself telling anyone who would listen about France. She wouldn't forget Le Pen or the man at the airport, the sound of the pistol next door, because they were underlying and disturbing aspects of France that were new to her. But France was wonderful. That's how it was. Full of sights and sounds that intrigued her. And overriding all of that, she noticed hats.

Hats! Imagine! More likely, she'd start talking about hats!

At the house, Richard was packing his suitcase. Marcel was whistling. "I'm driving to Avignon so Richard can catch a train to meet a cousin," he said. "In the Alps."

A jet suddenly streaked across the sky high above the valley.

"*La force de frappe,*" Clare said. Deep lines formed in a V between her eyes.

"At a spa," Richard nodded. "It's either too hot or too cold here. And I'm bored."

"Did you find your hat?" Libby asked.

"Who cares about a silly hat anyway?" Richard looked disgusted.

Marcel got into the car and started the engine, still whistling as he reached across to thrust open the door on the passenger side.

Acknowledgements

With thanks to Alistair MacLeod for accepting two of these stories ("A Country Weekend" and "Hello, Angel") for publication in the *University of Windsor Review* early on in my career. I did not know Alistair was the one who had accepted these stories until I met him in his group of students at the Humber School for Writers in 2006.

And also with appreciation to my colleagues at the Moosemeat Writers' Group. I joined the group in the fall of 2005 and was able to have some of the most recent stories critiqued there. I have also been fortunate to have participated in programs at the Banff Centre for the Arts, the Maritime Writers Workshop, and the Humber School for Writers.

I would like to acknowledge grants received from the Canada Council and the Ontario Arts Council many years ago which did not result in published books at the time, but helped me to serve what turned out to be a very long apprenticeship. For a long time, a Japanese proverb hung over my desk: "Even a thief takes ten years to learn his trade." I took much longer.

Margaret Hart, HSW Literary Agents, with her patience and humour, is a pleasure to have as my agent. I am fortunate to have had Luciana Ricciutelli work with me on my manuscript. She is a fine editor.

Thanks to Ian Wallace who has never wavered in his encouragement, ongoing support, and helpful comments. For editorial feedback on all of my manuscripts combined with constructive comments, I am grateful to Paula de Ronde. And to Brydon Gombay for the title and years of thoughtful conversation. To Larry Crackower for words of legal wisdom.

Thanks also to my daughter, Andrea, who took my work as a writer seriously from the time she was a teenager. And to my son, Phil, for his spirit of adventure that fuelled many discussions. To all the Farnsworth family of artists who have shared so much with me.

With thanks to all my friends who have waited forever for my books to be published and have never given up the belief that they would be. You are numerous and to mention some is to risk overlooking others. Even so, I wish to include a few names here: Don Heald, Joy Kogawa, Ruby Trostin, Michèle Chicoine, Lee Gold, Elizabeth Greene, Ray Bennett and my sister, Stephanie Farnsworth, have been there for conversation around the writing and creative process and also at times have read segments of my work.

Thanks also for friendship that made the ongoing struggle possible to Carol Findlay, Ray and Shirley Spaxman, Gwen McMurrich, Mark Sherman, Nicole Gombay, Larry Crackower, Gene Simon, Nelson and Catherine Priske, Anne Redpath, Margaret Arthur, Dianne Mesh, Ray Thompson, Ron Gold, Ila Rutledge, Liisa Tienhaara, Vince van Limbeek, Richard Bishop, Susan Walker, Deb Wallace. *Je me souviens.* Yes. Myrna Friend, Austin Clarke, Bev Wybrow, John Wilkinson, Rosa Shand, Paul Petrie, Bas van Fraassen, Joan Burrell, Clare May, Jean Dorr, Huong Pham, Jane Marvy, Joan Robson, Maryka Sule, John and Diane Cosser and all their family, Malcolm Savage, Helen Filion, SG, and others. And to my long-time neighbours, Ken and Greg.

Mary Lou Dickinson graduated with a Bachelor of Arts from McGill University and a Master of Library Science from the University of Toronto. She worked for many years as a crisis counsellor. Her fiction has been published in the *University of Windsor Review, Descant, Waves, Grain, Northern Journey, Impulse, Writ,* and broadcast on CBC Radio. Her writing was also included in the anthology, *We Who Can Fly: Poems, Essays and Memories in Honour of Adele Wiseman.* Mary Lou Dickinson grew up in northern Quebec and has lived for many years in Toronto.